SUNDROPS

SUNDROPS

.. ❧ ..

J. A. Springs

Always for J.M.S. First

This book is dedicated to my son Jordon. I wish you the best.

1

Leon "Sunny" Bright drove his car southbound out of downtown Atlanta. He was heading down Capital Avenue on his way to South Atlanta. The south side of Atlanta was not his usual hangout but he was going to meet up with somebody that he had met a month ago while out on the basketball court in a park in Eastpoint, Georgia not far from South Atlanta.

During that time, he and his people had decided to go out in that direction searching for a game of pick-up. They played the locals in the area in a two on two game of basketball to eleven points with the stakes at a hundred dollars a point plus another fifty dollars per point for the point difference at the end. Sometimes it was a lot more per point. That depended a lot on what was agreed upon at the onset of the game.

Sunny and two others of his friends were good as a two man team, with one friend acting as backup and watcher. Sometimes things got a little bit hairy when your opponents were facing an eleven point loss with a payout of sixteen hundred and fifty dollars or more.

When things went good, Sunny could wind up with about a five hundred dollar payout from a fifteen to twenty minute game of basketball. There were always hopefuls on the sidelines waiting for their turn to give it a try; a chance that might end up leaving them broke. That was cool by Sunny. He liked taking other people's money. It was a quick hustle that was not illegal, per se, and was less likely to get him killed like dealing in drugs would.

Sunny pulled up a side street and paused at a traffic light. He watched the young black boys as they prowled through their territory. No gang signs were thrown around and no colors were noticeable but that meant very little. These young black males knew their own from a quick sideways glance. They could tell the difference between some kid just walking the block and a young bull strutting in new territory trying to find trouble.

Atlanta was an equal opportunity thug community. The young bull didn't necessarily have to be black. That essential clue that served to point out the difference between harmless and a threat was hard to pin down and quantify but it was extremely important for survival on the streets.

You were relatively safe to walk the streets of Atlanta and would hardly get a cross word come your way, even if you were from uptown. This wasn't a guarantee of safety but again, as long as you weren't that 'young bull' with that certain *something* in your step, then you were just fine.

Sunny knew enough about the streets of Atlanta, just as the sun knows its path across the sky. He was aware enough to know where he could and could not go. Where he would and would not get confronted. When he shouldn't be in some certain areas and more importantly, when to get the hell out of others.

Where he was currently going wasn't a bad part of town. Atlanta was more diversified than that. Violence on the city streets took no notice of the area of town that it wanted to occur on. Not in this city. It was all equal opportunity.

The house that Sunny pulled up on was large, but not so much by the city standards. Atlanta was an old city, still full of life and remembrance of the old days. If an old home could be restored, then it was. This meant that there were hundred year old homes within the city limits with well over three thousand square feet of living space in them.

A lot of the older, South Atlanta homes were bereft of a driveway, so Sunny parked on the street, in front of the dark green, two story house. He got out of his car, hit the key fob to lock the doors and walked up the short walkway to the front door of the house.

The porch was as wide as the front of the house. Another aspect of the older homes prevalent in the city. An old porch swing hung suspended from the ceiling of the porch. The old white paint on the wooden swing matched the dark green paint that had been applied to the wooden siding of the house. They were both peeling badly. Other than the old paint covering the house, the residence was in a reasonably well kept state of repair.

Sunny didn't have to knock. He was called right into the house when his footsteps on the wooden porch announced his presence to the occupant. He walked in without waiting because of that.

'Hot-Lanta' was in full effect outside, the sun's fiery embrace driving the midday temperature settling in at a lazy ninety-one degrees so far that day. It wasn't promised to get hotter but that hardly mattered, as far as making the heat more oppressive went.

It wasn't the heat that was the enemy of the true southerner — even for the city dwelling southern boy or southern belle. It was the humidity in the south that deserved to be cursed back into the bowels of hell. Due solely to that thrice damned humidity, Sunny was sweating already and all he had done was walk to the house from the car.

Sunny mopped the sheen of perspiration from his brow and his short, crew cut hair. His light brown skin marked him as a member of that ubiquitous black sect known as 'high-yella' (pronounced as spelled) or 'redbone', depending on exactly which part of the south you were in. Atlanta tended to lean on 'redbone' while cities that lay to the west were more apt to use the appellate of 'high-yella'.

This southern home was old, so it had, what some older folks referred to as, a drawing room. It was complete with functional pocket doors. This is where Sunny found the individual who had called him into the house and who Sunny had come to see.

Anthony "Duke" Williams was sitting on the couch. He was wearing a wife-beater t-shirt and a pair of boxers. An afro pick was parked in the back of his head and the signature clenched fist listed awkwardly to the left. It looked as if it would fall out at any moment but it hung on — suspended right there — for dear life. Sunny smiled when he saw Duke.

Anthony couldn't tell Sunny how he got the nickname Duke. It had started up one summer in his early youth and it had seemed to stick to him like the summer humidity made your clothes stick to you. Sunny owed his nickname to his bright colored skin and to his last name actually being Bright. Duke waved Sunny to a chair on the opposite side of the room across from the double pocket doors. Sunny took the seat and waited for Duke to get off of his cell phone.

Duke soon put down his cell phone after ending his call. He placed it on the coffee table, next to two other cell phones. He leaned back on the couch and spread his arms wide across the back of it.

"Hey, I'm glad you made it, man," said Duke in way of a greeting to Sunny.

"Well you did ask me to get her by twelve," said Sunny as he glanced at his watch that was not there. "It's only 'skin-thirty' so I made it."

Duke laughed. Those individuals growing up in the south placed only minimum regard to being exactly on time. Things moved a bit slowly in the south. Southerners were said to even be 'late for their own funeral'.

"You're funny. Get over here," he said as he patted his lap.

Sunny stood up and walked over to Duke. He had to bypass the table that was positioned before the couch and sidestep until he was in a position where he could sit on Duke's lap. Duke put one army around Sunny's waist and dropped his other hand on Sunny's knee.

"You lookin' good," Duke said to Sunny.

Sunny wanted to be serious and say something cool and impressive, but he found that to be just a little bit difficult with Duke's hand roaming up and down his leg. The other hand causing him to have goose flesh as it whispered up and down his spine. These things only served to distract the hell out of him. Because of that, what Sunny finally managed to say was neither cool nor was it at all impressive.

"You look...comfortable," he managed with a grin on his face.

"Boy, you funny," Duke replied with a smile.

Duke stopped his hand at the back of Sunny's neck. He pulled him in close and kissed him passionately. Sunny felt himself partly melt from the heat in that kiss. Just like he felt he was melting from the sun when he was outside. He liked men that took the lead and knew what they wanted. He liked thugs and Duke was an old bull; as thuggish as they came. He slipped his tongue into Sunny's mouth and used it to start a fight with Sunny's tongue. The kiss ended up being over before Sunny even knew that it began. One of Duke's phones had called for attention and he broke off the kiss to answer it.

"What's up, man," Duke spoke into the receiver.

Sunny couldn't make out what was being said on the other end of the call but he wasn't nosey enough to care, either.

"...Nah, my man's just fell through and we 'bout to go ball at the park...'aight," said Duke into the receiver as he hung up the phone.

Sunny wasn't tempted to ask whom Duke had just spoken to on the phone. He wasn't that kind of boyfriend. He was fine with letting Duke have his space and privacy. Sunny had never been one of those insecure people who questioned every move made by his significant other.

Duke patted Sunny on his ass and lifted up his knee. Sunny got the hint. He got up and watched Duke rise from the couch while adjusting his boxers around his semi-hard member. Sunny unconsciously licked his lips and Duke smiled at him. He motioned toward the back of the house and started walking out of the drawing room, toward his own bedroom.

Sunny watched as the man in front of him continued to move. The muscles in his back and legs rippled beneath the dark chocolate skin. His powerful arms. Sunny wanted to reach out and run his hands along those strong, capable arms and have them wrap around him as he cupped those sculpted buttocks of Duke's in his hands. He couldn't help but think that Duke was fine as hell — the sexiest black man that he'd seen in a long time.

Duke led the way into his bedroom and Sunny followed. With a wave of his hand, Sunny shut the door securely. At another wave of Duke's hand, he claimed a spot on the edge of Duke's bed as while continuing to watch Duke getting dressed. Soon, they would both head out to the park down the street. The plan was to spend a few hours out there on the basketball court and then...who knows?

There weren't any definite plans on how they were planning to burn through the remainder of the sunlight after they wore themselves out playing basketball. Sunny didn't much care. To him, just being able to spend some time with Duke was all he wanted for now. For all he cared, they could watch a movie and chill for the remainder of the day. Sunny was partial to that idea, anyway.

Duke pulled on a pair of baggy shorts and an oversized, white T-shirt over the undershirt that he was already wearing. He went to the closet to get something for the court, and as he opened the closet door, a couple of bags fell out. Duke caught one of the bags and tossed it to Sunny, who caught the pound of bagged marijuana in both hands and looked at it.

"Yeah," began Duke, "I scored a few pounds of some premium gas a few days ago. With what I got, I can cop 'bout twenty bands or maybe even thirty depending on where I can unload this shit. Definitely thirty bands in North Atlanta."

Sunny knew that meant about twenty to thirty thousand dollars. It was impossible even to contemplate coming up on that much money at one time. It wasn't that he couldn't understand how anyone in the drug game could come up with that amount of money; it was just that *he* had never personally *seen* that much money at one time.

Duke pulled down one of the many shoe boxes from off the top of the closet and popped off the lid. Sunny eyed rolls of twenties and hundred-dollar bills secured with rubber bands. Presumably they were in groups of a thousand. That was the normal amount that you'd find trap money rolled in. With the rubber band wound round it, the rolls of money received their distinct name of 'band-o's' in the hood. Duke pulled out three rolls and looked over at Sunny.

"How you strapped for cash, bro?" asked Duke.

Sunny smiled and waved his hand as if to say "I'm good."

Truth be told, a few dollars was about all the money that Sunny had. He wouldn't get paid again from his part-time job for another week. He also didn't have any pick-up games lined up, either. The money in that shoe box looked tempting enough, but he didn't want things to get twisted between him and Duke. He wasn't after Duke's money. He wanted *Duke*. Also, while a box full of money looked like it would be a nice thing to have, the troubles that came with that trap money weren't worth the price, as far as Sunny was concerned.

Duke stood over Sunny and coolly peeled off five, hundred-dollar bills from the roll in his hand. He slipped this into Sunny's limp fingers at the same time he took the brick of weed from him. He put the rest of the cash into the pocket of his shorts and then he put the shoe box full of trap money and the weed back on the top of his closet, closing the closet behind him.

Sunny continued to watch Duke get ready. He knew better than to expect that Duke had gone to the closet for a pair of shoes. Duke pulled a shoe box from the top of his dresser. There were six matching boxes stacked beside it. All of the boxes contained brand new pairs of the same name brand sneaker. Same color. Same size.

Sunny had seen it before and thought that it was wasteful. Duke never wore the same pair of shoes twice — ever. Sunny had asked about it once and found out that when Duke was growing up, shoes were a luxury. At one point, he'd kept the same pair of shoes for almost three years before he got new ones. He'd only had the one pair, and his eventual new pair were hand-me-downs from a female relative.

Duke told Sunny about that shortly after they got to know each other and he said, "when I got to the point where I didn't have to wear the same pair of shoes again, that was when I began feeling like my own man."

Sunny hadn't known what to say about that and so he wisely chose to say nothing at all. It wasn't his place to judge how another man spent his money. He was, at least, proud of the fact that Duke would either give the old shoes away to a kid in the neighborhood who needed them, or he would donate them to a charitable cause. Regardless of that, the habit of Duke's to always rock brand new footwear, each and every day, only served to let Sunny know that Duke had money to burn.

THEY walked to the park from Duke's house. It was not far to the park from where Duke lived. It was only three blocks away and it gave them the opportunity to stop at the corner store to pick up drinks. Staying hydrated in the sweet southern heat of Atlanta was a requirement, not a luxury or a choice. Every summer in the city, you could catch news reports of people succumbing to the oppressive heat. Duke and Sunny were smart enough to get sports drinks that would hydrate them as well as provide the necessary electrolytes.

The courts were not as busy as they would get later on in the day toward the early evening hours when the temperature would fall to a reasonable level of two degrees cooler than hell, the sun's retreat casting a gentler touch. A few cars took two parking spots. Music was blaring from a few of the cars. It was the rhythmic sounds of urban music that filled the air. It was the sounds of the park that you would expect to hear in a major metropolis with a moderately wealthy, African American majority.

Most of the girls present were scantily clothed. Their male counterparts wore courtier that worked as the plumage of the peacock, meant to draw the eyes of potential mates. In this heterosexual environment, men like Sunny were a rarity. There were other venues around the city where his type of individual gathered around to perform the complicated dance that would attract the attention of a potential mate.

Sunny didn't care about that scene or any other. He didn't care to be out and about, eyeing the abundance of naked flesh being peddled under the hot city sun. His man had his attention. He had eyes for Duke alone. The way that the thick, ropey muscles bunched together, rubbed against one another. The way that they worked back and forth. Sunny loved the sight of him.

There was so much to see, starting with that wicked, lopsided smile, that promised trouble or a quick laugh. The way that the sweat rolled down his neck and onto his shirt, forging a path between his thick pectoral muscles. Sunny would have eaten up that chocolate sundae standing in front of him any day of the week.

They played more than a few games. Sunny and Duke played as a single, two-man team or as members of a larger team doing a full-court press when they had enough willing players. The sun began its slow descent from its position of prominence. Shirts had already been lost, tossed off to the side of the court and neglected during the need to push back and forth on the court in the early evening heat. That had happened hours ago, and as the sun dropped, so did that infernal temperature.

Sunny and Duke took a late break in the waning, orange-tinted, early evening. They had been at the game, on and off, for the better part of four or five hours. The sun had already dipped below the horizon and the low buzz could be heard all down the street as the sodium gas-filled street lamps started coming on, illuminating the city's path after the sun's departure.

Fifty years ago, the kids knew that they had to have their asses already in the house by the time the streetlights came on. It was not like that anymore. The panthers prowled the forest floor looking either for some 'cut-up' or looking to *cut up*. One of those meant 'acting a fool,' the other one was a loose description of a more pleasant repast and in most cases, it was enjoyed by two individuals. Only the daring increased that count of participants to fill the depths of their need.

Sunny slapped the lid back on his sport drink bottle. He put it down beside him on the picnic table and regarded Duke. They were near one of the many picnic tables scattered around the park.

"Have you ever thought about giving it up?" Sunny asked Duke.

Duke gave Sunny a confused look and sat down on the picnic table with his feet up on the bench. He had been staring at some girls seated at a nearby table.

"Give what up?" he eventually replied.

"You know...the 'game'?"

Duke put his hands behind him and leaned back so that he was lying down on the surface of the table. He looked up at the court lights overhead, and at the insects that were swarming around the lights in busy, dizzying clouds. They were inside the city limits — less than fifteen — maybe twenty minutes, outside of downtown — and the bats were still active, diving into that swarming mess of insects, snagging their next meal.

"I ain't thought about it. I guess I'm just gonna keep trappin' till I die," he said eventually; absently. There seemed to be a lack of concern for the future in his response.

Sunny heard the resignation in his voice, and a part of him got angry. There were too many black males being caught up in that cycle of violence, drugs, and money. Sunny hadn't known Duke longer than a month, but he knew that Duke was too smart for his own good. That sometimes appeared to be the crux of the matter. The smart ones got denied the opportunities that they needed to get out of that cycle of poverty. They would then choose the only escape they knew from the ravages of indiscriminate poverty. They would end up picking up a gun. They eventually became a part of the system — and the 'system'.

"You have so much more potential than this, Anthony. You've got the money to pay for college and you've got the brains to succeed," said Sunny.

"Call me 'Duke,' bro. I don't too much care to be called Anthony no mo'," said Duke as he sat up and looked down at Sunny on the bench beside him. "I also don't wanna do nothin' different den what I'm doin' right now."

Sunny frowned. "This lifestyle is going to catch up with you one day. You can't avoid it forever. You should get out of it while you still can."

Duke smiled at Sunny, and that was enough to send a small shiver of pleasure racing up and down his spine. His straight, white teeth seemed to shine in the glow of the streetlamp and contrasted beautifully with his hot, dark skin. Sunny had to fight to keep his mind on the conversation at hand.

"You know why you shouldn't take life so serious, Sunny?" Duke asked him.

"I don't. What do you mean?" Sunny responded in confusion.

Duke leaned over and pressed his open palm against the back of Sunny's neck and gave him a little shake as he spoke.

"You shouldn't take life so serious cause *none* of us get out of it *alive.*"

Duke's hand dropped away as he stood up from the picnic table and stretched. He let out a hearty laugh at his own joke while his joints popped. He moved away from the table and started walking off on his own, without waiting for Sunny to join him before he headed out of the park. He was done playing basketball for the evening and he was ready to head home, eat, and find something else to get into.

Sunny bounced up from the bench and ran to catch up to Duke. "Duke, I'm serious. You know you can't keep trappin' forever. There are *no* old folks retired from the 'game.'"

"Yeah, bro. I gots you. You ain't told me nothin' I ain't already know and peeped out. Da trap game got an expiration date. So does everythang in this world. It be like dat."

"But you really don't have to stay in the game until that time."

Duke turned around to face Sunny and spread his arms out wide. "What I *gotta* do? What I *should* do? Who knows what it is, 'cause I sure don't; 'sides, dere ain't nothin' else I'm good at."

"Have you tried to do anything else?" asked Sunny.

Duke flashed him that winning smile again. Sunny was not falling for it this time. Duke cocked his head to the side. "What chu got in mind for me to do? You think I'll be able to get dat degree and work in somebody's building as a good little cog in a wheel? Nah, man. Dat shit ain't for me at all."

"There's more out there than working in some big office building."

"Oh yeah?" asked Duke. Duke thrust out his chin toward Sunny as his arms dropped back down to his sides.

"What chu doin'? How you makin' bread, playa? 'Cause from where I'm at, I don't see nobody payin' me enough to keep me dripped up in new sneakers. Nobody keepin' me icy but me," said Duke as he gripped his gold chain.

"There ain't nobody gonna put dis kind of cake on my plate," Duke finished, while pulling the wad of cash out of his pocket.

Duke peeled off a few twenty-dollar bills and threw them up in the air. He laughed when the girls who had been sitting at the next picnic table jumped up, and damn near fought one another, grabbing the discarded bills. Duke pulled off a few more bills. These he balled them up and threw them, one by one, at the girls as they pushed and shoved one another trying to retrieve those first few bills off of the dirty ground. As they picked up the bills, each and every one of them, they lost a little of their dignity in return. It was not a new exchange. People of all shapes, creeds, color — everyone desperate; they had all given up one for the allure and prestige that the other promised.

That unspoken trust between the seeker and the changer of fate, promised of big dreams coming true. If you could get enough, it promised to open up the world for you. Problem was, there was never going to be enough.

The real gift it gave to you was the desire for more. The more that you got, thinking it would make you happier, then the more that you needed — or wanted. It was a vicious, black cycle. It would continue being a vicious, black cycle until the end of time.

Sunny never wanted to get caught up in that endless dance with money. It was the headiest drug that there ever was. It was worse than anything that man could inject into his veins or put up his nose or introduce into his body in some other way. Sunny didn't want a part of that and had other plans for his life. He decided to tell Duke his own plans for the future.

"I'm going to see about getting a gig at the Laugh Factory downtown," Sunny informed Duke.

"Now that sounds fly. I can get wit' dat shit. You are a funny brotha' sometimes," said Duke with a little laugh.

Sunny was about to say something more, but Duke stopped him. They were just shy of stepping off the sidewalk and moving into the parking lot. Duke had his arm out to stop Sunny from walking any farther. A car pulled to a stop in their path and the two young black males in the car were looking pointedly at Duke. Duke was facing the passenger of the car.

"What's up, nigga?" asked Duke.

The black male in the passenger seat threw his head back.

"What's good, '*folk*'?" said the passenger.

"Don't go flaggin' dat shit up here, partna'. We don't walk dat shit down here in the South-A."

'Folk' was a gang euphemism. Sunny understood *that* much at least. He also knew that Duke had no dealings with street gangs. He was not a member, and even if he sold his drugs to them, he would not put up with them invading the area that he lived in. No one in the city challenged him on this.

Duke didn't like gangs for simple reasons. Most times, they initiated senseless violence for reasons as stupid as wearing a different color. They didn't discriminate against age most times. Lastly, being in one would have limited his independence. Duke valued his freedom and independence.

The guy in the passenger seat looked over at the driver of the car and hooked his thumb out at Duke. "Ya hear dat fool?"

Duke pulled his shirt up and put his right hand on the butt of the semi-automatic pistol in his waist band. "You got a problem, den pull out a pole, *fool*. I'm ready to hear some clappin' with no hands. If you ain't wit' it, nigga, spin da block."

The driver of the car put the transmission into gear and slowly pulled off. Both the passenger and driver continued to watch Duke as they pulled away until they were completely out of sight. They stopped at the entrance to the parking lot, waited a few seconds, and then pulled off in a squeal of tires and smoke.

"Dat's what I thought," Duke said to no one in particular.

Sunny was surprised. He hadn't seen Duke pick up the gun at the house. He was certain that Duke had walked out of the house with no heat whatsoever. Duke looked over his shoulder as he pulled the Glock out of hiding. Some kid, that Sunny had barely noticed earlier, came over to Duke and took the gun from him. The kid could not have been much more than thirteen or fourteen years old, and he ended up disappearing into the crowd of onlookers that had gathered around behind them during the encounter. Sunny was tempted to ask after the gun and the kid that had taken it away, but he thought better of it and left it alone. Instead, he asked who the men were in the car.

"Dem two fools is shooters dat work wit' a dude named 'Black Vic'. A fool I been beefin' wit fo years," said Duke in response. "Him and his boys — dey nothin' but bark when you show 'em dat pole."

Sunny was not so sure if they were all bark. He saw the glint of a killer in the eye of the passenger. That was definitely a part of the game that Sunny wanted to avoid. He didn't think that posturing was worth a life. He had no shame in backing out of a pointless fight that was more likely to harm both sides rather than just the one.

He would stand his ground for justice. The right thing. Protecting the weak. Taking care of his own. Those were the real things that he felt people should die for. Things that they had a right to die protecting and a stake and investment in that would bring a positive dividend. Pointless sacrifice for the sake of a perceived slight was another waste that Sunny could not justify.

SUNNY didn't say anything else on the short walk back to Duke's house. They stopped at the corner store so that Duke could pick up some cigars for later. Those Optimos with the mango flavor were his favorites so he copped three of them. He also got himself a tall can of a heavy gravity beer. Even if Sunny had felt like drinking, he was not going to partake of that particular poison. He thought it tasted like diesel fuel and told Duke as much. Duke just laughed it off.

A wino was standing outside of the store when they left. He begged Duke for some money for something to eat. Duke ignored his request for alms and Sunny decided to reach into his own pocket to see what he could spare. Duke stopped him by taking hold of his arm. Duke spoke to the wino over his shoulder.

"Go tell 'em at 'Aunt Bee' I said 'put chu on,'" he told the wino.

Aunt Bee was a small mom-and-pop restaurant not far from where they were. If the wino told the management at the place what Duke had told them, they knew Duke would cover the cost. It was one of the many establishments that he used to launder his ill-gotten gains.

The wino thanked Duke for his generosity. Sunny watched as the man shuffled off to get the promised meal. Sunny wondered if the man would be able to find somewhere safe to sleep for the night.

Sunny cared; he cared and that was all there was to it. He knew that he could not save the entire world, but he would have tried, had it been in his power. He had been told a long time ago that 'a problem was no problem at all, if it could be solved with money.' Sunny could not understand where the money was that could take care of the social problems faced by his neighborhoods. Every block seemed to have a simple convenience store and the two products that they could not seem to keep on the shelves were cigarettes and alcohol. The demand for those two items was high.

North of Atlanta, he knew that you didn't see that shit in those neighborhoods. The residents up north had a scarcity of melanin compared to residents to the south, west, and east of Atlanta. For those individuals who lived up north with the same skin color as he, those haughty individuals acted like the other parts of Atlanta didn't exist. They had done their part for the community of African Americans when they — and it was to North Atlanta's credit that this happened — fought the city council to get rid of and reform the two major projects of Capital Homes and Carver Homes that were the last of their kind in the metropolitan area.

This *generosity* allowed the areas to be safely gentrified. Sunny wondered what was going to become of the communities that were just south of the city. He wondered where the winos, homeless, and other indigent residents of South Atlanta were supposed to go. What were the resources that were going to be made available for those that were unfortunate? Was it possible that anyone, besides himself, even cared?

This was the same group of cohorts who begged you to let them wash the dirty windows of your car while holding a beat-up rag and a busted bottle that you hoped contained window or glass cleaner but was likely just water. These were the same individuals who would wait at the gas stations right off the highways in the south of Atlanta and ask if you needed them to pump your gas for you so that they could hopefully get a little change in return. They stood at the bottom of the off ramps of the freeway with a handwritten, cardboard sign spelling out their troubles and hoping for a display of magnanimity.

Digging in trashcans for scraps and looking in gutters for the butts of cigarettes to take a couple of drags off, their dignity was cast aside in order that they could do what they needed to do to get what they wanted and needed to survive. That could easily be a chicken sandwich, a bottle of liquor, or a hit of some illegal substance.

Sunny pushed all of those thoughts out of his mind because it would end up spinning around in his head, in its repetitious circular logic, with no viable solution—at least not one that he was aware of. He knew that he was going to keep it in mind so that he could use it as social commentary at his gig — whenever he got one.

That was the best he'd be able to do based on the power for change that he held in his hands for now. He knew that it was not enough. Somehow, it was going to have to *be* enough for now. He was not planning on ever stopping, and someday he would be in a position to do much, much more.

Duke got Sunny back to his house and was able to scratch together a decent meal for the two of them. There were just enough ingredients between the cupboard and the refrigerator and just enough knowledge of cooking between Duke's ears to make him dangerous in the kitchen. Despite that, he put together something that impressed Sunny and made him appreciate the effort. Sunny definitely enjoyed the meal, but what made it so memorable was the thought and effort that had been put into it .... not to mention that he would get to eat that meal with that same person.

Sunny had brought a change of clothes with him to Duke's house. He hadn't made any assumptions but it didn't hurt to be prepared. Things seemed to actually work out in his favor, though. Duke asked him if he needed to get cleaned up after their workout, and Sunny told him he would.

Duke and Sunny took a shower together and cleaned up from their physical activities. Now Sunny desired a different type of physical activity, and he made sure that Duke was aware of his intentions.

They could not keep their hands to themselves, and they kissed, petted, and rubbed one another while making their way from the bathroom to Duke's room —just across the hall from the bathroom. It was *Duke's* house and his sister and mother lived with *him*.

Duke had been able to purchase the house, but he did so in his mother's name. He gave her the money that she needed for the downpayment and then he had continued to give her money and insisted that she make double payments until the house was completely paid off. Duke and Sunny didn't have to worry about being seen because Duke's sister was at her boyfriend's house and his mother was working an overnight shift at Emory Hospital in downtown Atlanta.

Duke pulled Sunny into his room. Sunny was ready for the kisses, and he responded to Duke in kind. His skin felt electrified when Duke's rough hands slid over him. Each touch stoked a fire within Sunny until his whole world was emblazoned. The conflagration coursed through his veins and burned a path along his nerves until it seared all rational thoughts from his mind, leaving him capable only of responding to the prompts that his body received from Duke.

Sunny felt a hand grasp roughly on his buttocks and draw him closer until skin touched skin. Sunny wanted more and honestly wondered if he was ready for more. He felt the hairs raise on his arms, his legs, his head. Duke parted his lips in a passionate kiss and Sunny yielded readily to the violation of his mouth. His tongue was pinned into submission. He was going numb, but he wanted — no, *needed*—to feel even more.

Sunny felt a hand around his waist and Duke guided him in a sensuous dance around the room. His mind spun in circles and each turn made his heart hammer violently against its cage of bone, cartilage, muscle, and flesh. Each beat pounded on the boundary of the chest that sought to contain it. The heart poured more than blood through his body; it pumped that *heat* deep into the recesses of his flesh and even deeper into his soul.

He fell, both literally and figuratively. He could not stay upright. His knees gave way, allowing the towering, classically cut Greek god the color of polished bronze, to fall upon the sea of linen behind him. Those hands kept pushing Sunny further and further away from consciousness; closer and closer to the edge of insanity. Those lips kept stoking the furnace, bringing that internal fire to the point where it would cause the star to collapse, consuming itself until it exploded outward.

Duke turned Sunny over. He was gentle but forceful. He was methodical. He was teasingly slow when he needed to be. The sword was finally sheathed. Duke drew it forth and together, he and Sunny entered into a sensuous rhythm. They danced, and oh, how Sunny enjoyed that dance. The waves crested. They broke against the rocky shore. The tide brought the sea level higher and higher and higher until...shivers rocked through their bodies as they crested the climax that they had worked so diligently to achieve.

This was the first wave, and it was followed by another wave and yet another, until the energy within the storm began to ebb and fade. The tide withdrew and the sword was drawn out. It took moments in silence before their breathing reverted to normal. Sweaty, hard bodies collapsed, one atop the other. The lingering warmth of the day's sunlight held within the night breeze, gently wafting through the open window and caressing their naked bodies. Sunny's eyes drifted closed as he lay in the summer evening calm. Duke was lying on his side, facing Sunny who was lying on his belly, his head on his crossed arms. Duke drew lazy circles on Sunny's flesh and watched as his muscular back trembled from the erotic touch.

The noises of summer crept in through the partially open window as they lay together. The cicadas made their presence known to the two of them. Cicadas are one of those southern phenomena that make themselves a part of the summer season, just like pitchers of sun brewed sweet tea, or lemon-aide with real lemon slices. They called out their incessant song and the lovers were lulled further into a sense of relaxation.

Duke drew the blankets over them both. He was soon fast asleep and left Sunny to wonder and dream at the magic of the summer evening. Sunny curled up beside Duke and watched his sleeping lover as he let the day replay in his mind. A lot had happened, and he watched the events play out as if he were a theatre patron.

Duke was amazing. He was handsome. He was self-assured. He was caring, in a way. He was the real deal. They had only known each other for a short time but he was feeling confident that he had made a good choice with his heart. He was worried about Duke staying in the game, but he hoped against hope that if he could make it as a successful comedian, he might just be able to convince Duke to leave all of the madness behind and get out of the game for good. The last thing that he wanted was to lose Duke to the game. He knew that he would be devastated if that ever were to happen. He was going to keep pressing Duke until he decided to give it all up—for good.

2

It was around nine in the morning by the time that Sunny finally walked through the front door. He just happened to come into the house as his father was walking past the front room, going into the kitchen. They greeted each other awkwardly in response to the abrupt meeting. He and his father had stopped trying to be comfortable as a family on the day that his mother passed away.

Sunny said something that day that his father had never tried to take the time to understand. Sunny's mother was on her deathbed when he decided that he didn't want her to go away without knowing her son in every way, every truth exposed. He told his mother that he was gay, and his father had overheard the conversation.

Sunny's mom confessed that she was already aware of his proclivity and that she still loved him. After hearing so potent of a revelation, his father seemed to drift away from him, day by day.

"Hey, Pops," said Sunny.

"Hey, son. Nice morning. It's supposed to be hot again today like it was yesterday," Peter replied.

Sunny wanted to scream. Speaking with his father had gotten stiff, and awkward. It was like listening to two rocks scraping against one another. It was rough, disjointed, incoherent. It was mostly just benign chatter used to chase away the uncomfortable silences. This worked only long enough for the silence to come crashing back even more noticeably.

Sunny desperately wanted to work past it but because of the truth hanging out there, naked and bold, this was the best that they would be able to manage, he thought. Sunny tried to make the communication work between them though.

"Dad, are we doing brunch?" Sunny asked his dad.

Before his mother had gotten sick with cancer, he and his dad would make brunch together on Saturday mornings and then call in his mom to join them.

"Yeah, yeah. Sure. Let's do that," said Peter with a smile slowly spreading across his pale face. Peter tossed his head to the side, his brunette bangs brushing against his hazel eyes. Peter was Caucasian and Sunny's mother was African American. That explained Sunny's light complexion.

They both walked off into the kitchen. Sunny opened the refrigerator and looked in while Peter searched the pantry.

"I don't see any eggs, Dad," said Sunny. "Or bacon," he added after a brief pause.

"Yeah, I don't see any pancake mix here, either. I'll run to the store," Peter offered.

Peter seemed to be loosening up at the thought of sharing brunch with his son. He appeared to be a little bit more chipper and it helped alleviate some of the tension between them, setting them both at ease.

"You want me to ride out with you?" Sunny asked.

Peter shook his head 'no' as he scooped up his car keys from the center of the kitchen table.

"Naw, I got it. I'll be back soon," he said as he headed toward the front door of the house.

Sunny shrugged his shoulders, resigned. His father was capable of picking up a few groceries on his own. As soon as his dad stepped out the front door, Sunny stopped worrying about his father. He had other, more pressing problems. He wanted to get cleaned up and get ready for the day. There was a lot that he wanted to get done. Now a part of those plans included maybe spending some time with his dad without the usual tension.

Sunny caught a quick shower. He was getting dressed and reciting the lines to his comedy routine when he saw his dad walk past his open bedroom door. He finished getting prepped and it wasn't long before he and his dad were cooking brunch together like they used to do. They worked in companionable silence for the first few minutes until each was set on the course of their particular path of culinary glory and so well underway that their minds could set the accomplishment of their task on cruise control.

Peter was the first to speak. "I heard some of your material for your comedy act when I walked past your room a bit ago. That's some pretty funny stuff, son."

"Thanks, dad. A lot of it I picked up from hanging out with the guys and Miranda."

Peter seemed to think. His gaze drifted off for a second before returning to the present. "Oh, Miranda? Your old school friend? How is she? I haven't seen her in a week."

"Now that you mention it, she's doing okay. She actually called when you were gone so I invited her over for brunch."

Peter smiled and said, "that sounds great. I wouldn't mind having her join us."

Peter finished cutting up some onions and was now dicing up tomatoes for the omelettes while Sunny checked on the bacon in the oven and got ready to pour the batter for the pancakes.

"Speaking of Miranda," Peter continued after a pause, "why aren't you two a couple? I mean you've known each other since middle school and you're thick as thieves. There's no separating you two!"

Sunny stifled his immediate surge of anger. His father knew full well why he had never pursued a relationship with Miranda. It was not due to any negative qualities. She may have been a little too trusting and too naive at times, but Sunny found those qualities endearing. So...no, it was none of that.

Miranda was the wrong sex. It was as simple as that. Nothing more. Nothing less. Without thinking, he was about to express his displeasure with his father in no uncertain terms, but luckily, he was interrupted by the sound of the front door bell.

Sunny picked up a kitchen towel from the counter. As he walked past his father, he put his hand on his father's shoulder and gave it a little squeeze, accompanied by the slight upturn of his full lips in a caring and gentle smile. "It wouldn't work between us, dad."

Wiping his hands, he began walking out of the kitchen, toward the front door to see who was calling on them on this early summer weekend morning. Sunny easily guessed it was Miranda.

Peter heard the two sets of feet coming down the hallway toward the kitchen. One set was coming at a fast pace and he braced himself, as best he could, for that incoming rush. A little, slight wisp of a dark-skinned girl rounded the corner and bounded into the kitchen. She was all energy and the space actually seemed brighter with her presence. Peter chalked it up to his imagination but appreciated it nonetheless.

Miranda threw her arms around Peter's neck and pulled his face down for a kiss on the cheek. Miranda was a full foot shorter than both Peter and Sunny.

"Good morning, dad," said the bouncing woman, her presence radiating warmth much like the morning sun.

"How many times do I have to tell you to call me Mr. Bright?"

"Maybe about two or three more times," said Miranda as she put a finger to her lips and cocked her head to the side.

Both Miranda and Peter laughed at the inside joke. Sunny moaned. She had called him dad since the day that she had met him. Now, after all of these years of knowing each other and growing comfortable with each other, it was their own little shared joke and official greeting.

Sunny came up from behind Miranda and resumed his station on the griddle. He flipped one pancake and then another. Miranda sniffed the air.

"That smells great," she said as she made her way to the kitchen cupboard to retrieve plates and cups for the place settings. "You know you two are the only guys that I know of who can cook."

Sunny laughed out loud and said jokingly, "You know that you're the only girl that I know of who *can't* cook."

Miranda punched him playfully in the arm. She finished setting the table and set out a container of orange juice that Peter had purchased earlier at the grocery store. She watched as Peter gingerly placed the omelettes on the plates, followed by Sunny adding pancakes and strips of bacon.

They were all in a joyful and joking mood as they sat down at the kitchen table to eat. They enjoyed the bounty of the prepared meal in the presence of those who they cared for. It was a picturesque scene—a cross between a Norman Rockwell painting and an Andy Warhol abstract; the warmth of a family setting mixed with the varied demographic, one black, one white, one mixed.

The only thing missing was a mother figure. In contrast to the wholesome family setting was the mirth and humor present in the moment; the irreverence necessary not to take life's hard knocks too seriously while still appreciating the beauty around you. Maybe there was room in that crossover for a love to bloom.

They ate. They laughed. They completed their meals and continued to sit enjoying each other's company. Sunny kept the small group smiling and laughing with his jokes. He was a natural at making people smile; at making people forget about their own personal worries and laugh at the foibles of the world. That was needed sometimes. That was a good thing.

Miranda was trying to control her laughter when she reached out and patted Sunny on the hand to get his attention.

"Can you go over some of your routine for the comedy club?"

Sunny smiled at her and his dad. It seemed like those present were eager enough to hear him try out his material, and so he did. He didn't think about the content of his material and what that might mean when taken out of context. He only thought about the material that he was delivering as a whole sum of the entire overall performance that he was eventually wanting to give to the audiences in the comedy club.

Sunny started out with the simplest part of his routine. He began at the introduction and deftly wove a verbal dance that had Miranda and his father struggling to catch their breath. Their initial, encouraging response motivated him to continue with his presentation.

Sunny started getting into the more serious subject matter that revolved around his sexual preferences, he noticed that his father's laughs were becoming less and less frequent and sounded forced instead of natural and easy. Finally, his father's laughs stopped altogether as he assumed a more solemn expression. Sunny could see his dad's jaw muscles working as he clenched his teeth. His eyes became cold and distant and Sunny's voice trailed off.

Miranda noticed the change in the atmosphere as soon as Sunny stopped talking. She could feel the change in the room as the uneasiness began to take on the qualities of a blanket and snuff out the previous joy that had filled the room. She looked between father and son and saw the tension, thick like smoke, that now hung between them. She became uncomfortable quickly enough now that she was fully aware of the change that had occurred.

"Why do you have to include that stuff about being gay?" Peter asked, his voice carrying an unintended weight.

"What do you mean, dad?"

"I mean, why do you have to throw that in everyone's face?" There was a hint of concern in Peter's tone, a subtle trace of something beneath the surface.

"I don't see how I'm throwing anything into anyone's face. Comedians share who they are and their personal experiences with their audience in order for the audience to be able to relate to them."

"I'm just saying that you can be funny without talking about all of that gay stuff."

"But that 'gay stuff' is who I am. I mean, who do you think I am, dad?"

"You're my son," said Peter emphatically. "That's who I think you are."

"But I'm also gay, dad."

Peter hesitated for a moment before responding, his gaze distant as if lost in thought. "You don't need to define yourself by any one thing, Sunny. You're more than that." Peter proceeded to continue, "You don't act gay. No one would be able to tell if you left that stuff out of your routine so why make that the majority of the stuff you talk about? I'm sure there's more you've seen that you can talk about."

"Are you kidding me?" asked Sunny.

Sunny was getting to the point where he wanted to slam his hands on the table but he just clenched his fists instead. "How are gay people supposed to act?"

"You know what I mean, son. I'm not trying to say something like that," said Peter as he closed his eyes and shook his head.

"No. I don't know what you mean. Tell me."

"Like — gay. The guys that act like women with the way that they talk, walk, and dress," Peter growled.

Sunny shook his head in disgust. "So I have to act like a flaming queen or it doesn't count? That's total bullshit!" Sunny said, his voice rising in frustration.

"I'm not trying to make it all about that, can't you understand?" Peter's voice rolled with a deeper rumble than it had before. "And you will watch your mouth when you speak to me!"

"I'm sorry, dad," Sunny mumbled. "I just never expected to hear such homophobic talk come from you."

"I am not homophobic," countered Peter defensively.

"Then what do you call it?"

"I...I —," stammered Peter before Sunny cut him off.

"Yeah, that's what I thought."

Sunny stood up and quietly cleared off the dishes from the table. The silence in the kitchen was heavy and every clink of a plate or utensil sounded that much louder as the quietude hung oppressively over the room.

Sunny finished the dishes and exited the kitchen. Peter had no idea how to go about fixing the situation. He didn't understand what had happened. Why it had happened. Without knowing, he had no hope of being able to start bridging the chasm between him and his son.

Miranda felt a little uncomfortable having been a witness to so intimate a family drama. She was glad that she had largely been ignored during the brief encounter. She stood up to go but didn't feel right with just leaving and saying nothing.

"Um...," she began hesitantly. "I'm gonna go and see how Sunny is doing, Mr. Bright."

Peter waved a negligent, dismissive hand. If he had even really heard what Miranda had just said to him then it failed to show. He also totally missed the fact that Miranda hadn't addressed him as 'dad' after how close they had become in the intervening years since Sunny and Miranda had first met.

There it was, right there between the two of them; he and Sunny. It was a wedge that was driving itself between the two of them, with society acting as the hammer to drive that wedge home—a wedge which threatened to break them.

It was going to rend them asunder and permanently divide both son and father if they could not find a way to get that wedge removed. Sunny could not do it alone because that would require him to deny his own sexuality. Peter could not do it alone because it would require him to face his own prejudices and biases. It was something that they were going to have to do together, though neither of them knew how to go about it.

3

Miranda found Sunny secluded in the relative safety of his room, a haven for him where the sun's tender fingers reached through the window blinds, casting a soft embrace over his solitude. It was one of the few places where Sunny could shut out the noise of the world. Sunny could find the separation from the world he needed occasionally here, in his own personal space. When that door to his room was closed, he could—temporarily, at least—block out all of the things on this mad planet that sought to beat against his sanity.

Sunny watched Miranda come into his room. She closed that sheltering shield behind her and came and sat on the bed beside him. Sunny smiled when Miranda leaned her head on his shoulder as if *she* were the one in need of comfort. He draped his arm around her shoulder and drew her closer.

"I don't know what to say," said Miranda.

"Then don't say anything," he replied.

"But I feel like I should say something."

Sunny scrunched up his nose. "Why should you have to say anything? This wasn't your fault and it shouldn't really concern you."

Miranda punched Sunny in his gut. He grunted in response and thought about pinning her down and tickling her. She would hate that, but he would love doing it, and right now he felt like she deserved it.

"It concerns me if it concerns you, goofy," she said.

Sunny decided that he was not going to tease her after all. He would save it for another day. She had come to cheer him up, after all, and he was going to let her try. He was not sure that she was going to succeed. Sunny's heart hurt because of what his dad had told him at the dining room table.

"My *loving* dad," said Sunny sarcastically.

"He does love you. You know that, right?" Miranda asked, concern showing in her expression.

"Yeah, I know. I know he loves me but it still hurts to be treated like an embarrassment and a mistake." Sunny turned from her, a slight frown clouding his features.

Miranda was worried about Sunny's perspective. "Wow. That's *really* how you feel he treats you?"

"How else can you explain it?" asked Sunny as he flopped back onto his bed, bringing Miranda down with him. "What I wouldn't give just to be accepted for who I am by that man."

"Why do you think he's like that? Do you think it has anything to do with being a retired, big bad Marine?"

"I don't think that's it at all. He's never been some kind of super masculine guy. He's just always been...my dad."

"Well, I think you should just let it go for now and concentrate on getting that routine together. I think you're on to something!"

"I plan on trying out for the open mic night at the Laugh Factory. I told my man about it and he thinks I should do it, too."

Miranda sat up. Sunny remained laying on the bed. She put her arm across Sunny and dug her chin into his chest. She had a shit-eating grin spread smack across her mug that Sunny was not sure that he liked.

"You got a *man*?" she squealed like a giddy school girl. "Tell, tell. I want to know all."

Sunny clasped his hands behind his head so that he could see Miranda more easily. "I met him a few weeks ago."

"You gotta tell," Miranda said with laughter in her voice behind that devilish smile. "So tell."

"I was out with Dan and Steve and we were hustling the courts in South Atlanta. We played a game with these two dudes. One was as tall as me. He was a dark, delicious looking piece of black man. After the game, he gave me his number and said to call him up sometime for a game of one-on-one."

"So obviously you called him."

Sunny could not keep the smirk from spreading across his handsome face, his cheeks reddening.

"Yes, I gave him a call, but his '*one-on-one*' consisted of...," Sunny's voice trailed off. He thought certain things should be left unspoken. Miranda squealed again. She rolled over and kicked up her legs while continuing to squeal.

"Okay, okay," said Sunny finally, laughing. "So what about you?" asked Sunny when Miranda had quieted down. "What's your love life looking like?"

Miranda bolted upright and turned, facing Sunny. She sat with her legs crossed and her arms on her knees. She had her feet in her hands. As far as Sunny was concerned, Miranda looked like a teenaged girl on a sleepover, trading secrets.

"You remember Victorious?" asked Miranda.

"Yeah, I think so."

"He's the guy from my senior year that I was going out with at the time."

"You mean that guy you told me had another two girls on the side? *That* Victorious?"

"Yeah, but it's not like that now."

"How you mean? That guy was a *dog* and I can't believe that you wanna give him another chance."

"He's different now —," began Miranda before being cut off.

"Different how?" Sunny interrupted while sitting up. "He was a dog *then* and he's probably *still* a dog. You deserve so much better than that."

Miranda leaned backward, staring at the ceiling. "And I'd *have* better, too, if he wasn't gay," she muttered.

"What?" asked Sunny.

"Nothing." Miranda spun around and bounced off the bed. "Are we still trying to get to the Laugh Factory tonight?"

Sunny slid forward to the edge of the bed, now wearing that same devilish grin that Miranda had been wearing on her face. His hand snaked out quickly and he pulled her in close to him. He wrapped one arm around her and used his free hand to tickle her.

"Try and stop me," he said over her raucous laughter.

Sunny decided to let her go. He didn't want to let her go just yet, but he figured that it would probably be in his best interest if he did. Miranda had declared, rather loudly, that she was going to wet herself if he didn't stop tickling her.

It took Miranda more than a few minutes to calm down to the point where she could curse freely at Sunny and declare him to be everything under the sun but a child of God. Sunny took her verbal abuse in good nature, as it was intended. He knew that she didn't mean any real harm.

They had been friends since middle school and they understood each other pretty well. Miranda had been the first person that he had ever told about his sexual preferences, and she had been his longest and staunchest supporter throughout all of the many challenges that he had faced since the day that the two of them had met.

Sunny gave his cell phone to Miranda. "I need you to take a video of me delivering my act. I want to do about ten minutes of material."

Miranda snatched the phone out of his hand in mock anger. "Only because I love you, jerk."

Sunny was going to use the clip to show the manager at the club. Even though he was going to perform at the open mic night, his ultimate goal was to get a regular slot in the rotation of performers. That was where he was going to make a name for himself and make an entrance into the business.

Sunny and Miranda watched the video a few times. She offered suggestions and he saw areas where he could improve as well. They recorded the video several more times until they felt that it was the best that it could be. Sunny then transferred the video onto a tablet and he and Miranda worked through his closet to get his wardrobe ready for his act.

They still had plenty of time to go before the club opened. Sunny went with Miranda over to her apartment so that she could find what she wanted to wear to the club. Miranda decided on a cute, backless, black cocktail dress but she didn't like any of the shoes that she had. She suggested that they could burn up some daylight by heading to a mall where they could find some appropriate shoes for her to wear with the outfit she had in mind.

Miranda wanted to purchase a new pair of shoes. Sunny was up for it. He just wanted to take it easy for the day until it was time to go to the club. The time flew by and they took it easy for most of the rest of the day. They stopped at Miranda's place to get ready for the. Sunny had dropped his clothes off at her place when they stopped there earlier that day.

Sunny and Miranda got to the club with time to spare. They ordered drinks and sat down to watch the show. There were a lot of funny people. Sunny was excited for the chance when he could join their ranks. The idea of that spotlight framing him on stage after hearing the MC call out his name was intoxicating in its own way. There was nothing quite like that initial rush of nerves, when you first hit the stage at the beginning of your set, that made you feel alive.

The two of them drank and they laughed. Several guys came through eyeing Miranda but were afraid to say anything, likely assuming that Sunny was her boyfriend. Miranda did little to encourage any of them because she was fine with the way things were.

When open mic began, Sunny was already on the list and was going to be heading up on stage as the second person to perform. He was nervous, as anyone *would* be. His stomach tightened with anxiety, and he felt a light sheen of perspiration on his forehead, despite the cool temperature inside the club.

Finally the time came where Sunny could make his presence known to the world. He got on stage and dominated the show. His material was fresh and so far from the norm that its very novelty drew the crowd in. He was on and off in about twenty minutes. That was twice as long as what was normally allotted on open mic nights, but the crowd didn't want to let Sunny go. They cried out and they clamored for him when he finished his initial ten-minute set.

The management of the club let Sunny continue that additional time; he was surprised at the reception that he had gotten and was damn grateful that the original set that he had come up with was just under half an hour. That extra material allowed him to give the audience what they wanted. They ate it up. There was no other way to explain it. Sunny had entered the zone and had delivered a knock-out punch.

Sunny came off the stage, high on the adrenaline rush and post coitus with his demanding audience. He was glowing like the star that he longed to be. He had experienced the joy of being on the stage and the tinge of regret from having to give up that spotlight afterward. From that moment on, Sunny knew what he was going to be, and nothing was going to keep him from reaching his goal.

Miranda gave Sunny a hug. She was so excited for him. They made their way over to the bar so that they could get a couple of shots each to celebrate. They downed the shots and sat back to enjoy the next few comedians to perform.

Sunny had to wait a little bit to see if he could get a moment to speak with the club manager while the reception he'd received was still fresh on the manager's mind. He had to wait until later into the evening when the manager was free from his obligations and could afford to devote some of his time to talk to Sunny about his success earlier that night.

Sunny and the manager spoke for about half an hour, and at the end of that time, Sunny was given the opportunity that he had been hoping for. His video from earlier showed the manager that Sunny had additional material that was just as funny and entertaining. Sunny could use this additional material to expand his repertoire to a full, one-hour set.

The manager asked for Sunny to come back during the daytime the following day so that they could take care of some administrative paperwork. That paperwork was going to be required when Sunny began having a regular set. A set that would be performed every week until it got to the point where Sunny needed to move on to continue growing as a comedian.

It was a good moment for advancing the goals of his chosen career path. Sunny felt that if he could convince his boyfriend to give up the game and find a safe gig to get into.... If he could get his father on board with the program, then everything would be perfect. Sunny's reverie was interrupted by the bartender vying for his attention.

"Yeah," Sunny responded to the tap on his shoulder.

The bartender slid a shot of liquor over to Sunny. Something clear. Miranda noticed and was intrigued and gave the new situation more attention.

"The guy over there at the other end of the bar bought you this drink," said the bartender. "He said you were good up there on the stage."

The bartender started to leave, then turned back to look at Sunny.

"You were real good, kid. Keep being real and the audience will love you for it," the bartender advised.

With that bit of advice, she moved on to take more orders and pour more libations for her thirsty customers. Sunny and Miranda looked down the length of the bar in the direction of the patron who'd bought

Sunny the drink. There was a tussle haired, Hispanic male with a single, large dimple in his right cheek. He raised his glass in salute to Sunny and downed his shot in one go.

Sunny returned the salute and did likewise with his own gifted shot of alcohol. The handsome young man continued to smile and stare at Sunny for a few more minutes before he turned around on his stool to face the nearby stage. He leaned his elbows back against the wood of the bar and seemed to settle in to enjoy the comedian onstage.

Miranda could not see Sunny blushing. The lighting in the club was low, and Sunny was facing away from her. He was staring at the back of his fan. Sunny immediately felt vindicated somehow because of that singular act of praise from such a good looking guy. He wondered absently, just for a moment, if he was gay. He just as quickly dashed the thought to stop his wandering imagination from indulging in inappropriate thoughts. Sunny had a man. Sunny's man was named Duke and Sunny was going to give the burgeoning romance its best chance at success and devote himself to it fully.

"He looks cute," whispered Miranda, elbowing Sunny.

Sunny smiled ruefully and turned away from his cute fan. He was definitely cute, thought Sunny. Then he reminded himself that Miranda made that comment, not him, so he didn't feel as guilty.

He faced Miranda and said, "yeah, but I got a man."

The smile that slid onto his face then seemed to make him glow all the more because of how his happiness radiated out into the world. Sunny and Miranda stayed the rest of the night until the club closed and then took a shared ride back to their homes. Sunny didn't get a chance to say thank you to the guy who had bought him a drink, but he hoped that he might see him again at the club in the future so that he could convey his gratitude.

4

Sunny was not able to see Duke for the rest of that weekend because Duke was busy. So Sunny spent that following Sunday hanging out with Miranda. Work ended up keeping Sunny from going to see Duke during the first half of that following week.

When Sunny's regular job was no longer a factor in being the reason he could not go to see Duke, it was Duke who told Sunny that he had obligations outside of town that he had to attend to. This entire sequence of events meant that Sunny had to wait until after his shift at work was over on Friday before he was able to go and see Duke again. He was more than excited at the prospect of being able to see that gorgeous chunk of man again.

Sunny kept biting his lip. He glanced at the clock. He was distracted to the point that his manager noticed and mentioned something to him about it. He and Miranda were coworkers at a bank. At their lunch hour, he said a few words to her about how the butterflies felt in his stomach. Sunny took Miranda home after work and it was almost as if she had barely closed the car door after getting out of the car at her house before he was speeding off down the street in a rush.

Miranda laughed and said a belated goodbye to the tail lights of the car as it barreled headlong towards the rendezvous that was causing so much anxiety in Sunny. Due to the anticipation of the meeting, Sunny decided to forgo stopping at his own house to shower off the work of the day and put on some regular street clothes.

Anything that was going to delay Sunny from reaching his goal of being able to see Duke after a week of being apart was quickly overcome in one way or another. He had even gone through the trouble of filling up the gas in his car on the evening previous so that putting gas in a hungry car would not end up becoming an unnecessary concern. Where there were stop lights, Sunny saw Duke waiting. Where there were yield signs, Sunny didn't see anything. He was, however, aware enough of his surroundings that he didn't have a traffic accident.

Needless to say, Sunny was almost bursting with anxious energy and he was very glad that when he pulled to a stop in front of his destination, the object of his thoughts was standing outside on the street. At first Sunny thought that Duke was waiting outside for him but he quickly realized that Duke was outside so that he could talk with the guy that was leaning on a car parked right there next to him on the street.

Sunny saw Duke look at him as he pulled up to park but it seemed to Sunny that Duke didn't recognize who he was, or he chose to *act* like he didn't recognize him. It was not until Sunny shut the car off and got out that recognition seemed to light up his face. Sunny was hoping that he was wrong, but it also appeared to him that a look of stricken panic flashed across Duke's features first.

Sunny closed his car door and walked over towards the two men. Duke began speaking to the guy on the car again and from what Sunny could hear, he had picked the conversation back up where the conversation had cut off when he got out of the car.

"All I fuck wit is dem Zannies and that gas, bro. If you talkin' weight with anythang else, I ain't got it, Black Vic."

Sunny watched the guy named Black Vic as he sized up Duke to see if he was shooting straight with him. Sunny didn't like the glint of trouble that he saw in the man's eyes. Sunny got close enough that he was going to say something in greeting to Duke but Duke cut him off before he could form any words.

"Sup, brah? Head on up to the porch, I'll be there after I'm done hollerin' at my man here, Black Vic."

Black Vic looked over at Sunny and greeted him with a head bob.

"So, this yo homeboy you was tellin' me 'bout? Y'all chillin' tonight?" Black Vic asked Duke as he continued to look at Sunny as if he was somehow familiar to him.

Sunny picked up on that immediately and shuffled through his own memories of faces and names to see if he could place the man that was standing in front of Duke. He could not place the face of the clean shaven, young black male with dreadlocks. He could not remember ever seeing the guy before. The only name that popped into his mind was tied to the two young guys that had driven past him and Duke as they were leaving the park a few days ago.

Sunny continued to walk on by the two of them when Black Vic reached out and stopped him by touching him on his arm. Sunny stopped walking and looked first at the hand on his arm and then at Black Vic as he slowly removed his hand from Sunny's arm and squinted as he looked in his face more intently.

"I done seen you 'round somewhere before," said Black Vic to Sunny.

Duke just stood to the side and continued to watch the interaction between the two men.

"Sorry. I don't know you, dude," said Sunny.

Sunny was not sure if he wanted to be upset at the guy or not, for having touched him. The irritation was not hidden from his voice though or his face and Black Vic raised his hands up slowly while an ugly, oily looking grin caused his gold cased teeth to show.

Black Vic squinted again as he leaned closer to see Sunny's features. He huffed after a second — as if he was realizing something. He nodded his head and as his hair bobbed up and down, he leaned back onto the car behind him, parked on the street, and crossed his arms.

"You know a chick named Miranda?" Black Vic asked Sunny.

It was Sunny's turn to squint then, as he forced himself to recall, even harder, a face that he had never seen before. "Yeah. She and I go way back. How do you know her?"

"I'm hittin' dat piece, dawg."

Understanding dawned on Sunny's face as his mouth opened up into the shape of an O. "*You're* Victorious?"

"Yeah, but only my moms and gran call me dat."

"Oh, okay," said Sunny in response.

Sunny didn't know what else to say to the man and so he said nothing. Black Vic was quick to fill the silence before it became awkward.

"Tell Miranda I said, 'wus up?'," said Black Vic.

Sunny nodded. "Okay. I will. Next time I see her."

Sunny turned back to the house and slowly ambled off after one final look back over his shoulder. Black Vic watched Sunny walk off and the smile on his face got much bigger.

"So, dat's yo dawg? The one you gonna kick it wit' tonight?" Black Vic asked Duke.

Duke glanced over his shoulder at Sunny sitting on the porch and then looked back at Black Vic. He replied slowly. Deliberately. Trying to determine if there was some hidden meaning in the question and, having found none readily apparent, he answered slowly.

"Yeah...why ya ask?"

"You know yo man's a fairy, right? He's tight wit' my girl and I knew I seen dat face somewhere before. He's on her Gram and Facebook. The guy's a full fledge fairy. Pink skirt and all dat."

Duke's hands balled up into fists. He leaned forward and an ugly look came upon his face. "So what chu sayin', huh?" he asked Black Vic.

Black Vic threw his hands up in defense and chuckled as he sought to lean further back away from Duke's aggression.

"I ain't sayin' nothin', nigga. I'm just tellin' you that...," Black Vic began then paused as he looked intently at the heavily breathing man in front of him. "Wait," he began again as his hands slowly fell away to his sides and he leaned in close to Duke. "You *already* knew? So it's like dat, huh, nigga?"

Duke tried his aggressive tactic again but was failing to make any impact this time. He gained no ground with his threatening posturing towards Black Vic.

"The fuck chu say, nigga?"

"Hey, man," said Black Vic, again raising his hands.

When Black Vic raised his hands this time though, he didn't raise his hands in fear or to ward off an attack.

"It's cool. You wanna smoke on dat meat pipe den dat's yo business. I don't give a fuck if you takin' it up da ass, brah," said Black Vic laughing.

Duke pulled up his shirt with his left hand and made a grab at the gun that was in his waistband. "The *fuck* chu say, nigga? I ain't no fuckin' fag and if you say dat shit again, I'll cock dis pole and smoke yo bitch ass!"

Black Vic put his hands slowly into his own pockets.

"It's cool," Black Vic said slowly. "I don't want no smoke, Duke. *We* good, but chu better check up on yo bitch. I don't think he likes what he heard," Black Vic continued as he laughed lightly and got into the car he was leaning on.

Black Vic tapped the shoulder of the guy in the drive's seat and they slowly pulled off. Black Vic pointed his finger at Duke as if it were a pistol. He imitated pulling the trigger and laughed out loud. Duke watched them drive off until he noticed Sunny coming off of the porch out of the corner of his eyes.

"Hold up, man," called out Duke as he moved to intercept Sunny and block his movement. "Where you goin'?"

Sunny just looked at Duke as if Duke had just told him that he believed that the tooth fairy was real. He laughed at the choice of words in that thought — fairy. Sunny was to the point where the focus of his vision had constricted to a singular point. He could hear the blood coursing along the byways in his body. Rushing in his ears. The sound of the pumping blood in his ears reminded him of the dark waves crashing against the shore of a beach at the head of a storm.

Sunny's nostrils flared as he breathed in and out and his fists clenched and released. He was ready to strike out. The object that he wanted his fist to connect with was standing right in front of him.

Those high cheekbones. The narrow jaw and full lips. Those liquid brown eyes that he used to want to be seen by everyday. All of this was what he was tempted to try and destroy with his own hands as he lashed out, but he didn't do it. Sunny took a deep breath and his shoulders gave up their high position. The muscles along his back lost their tension as his anger drained. His eyes widened and lost their narrow focus. All of this happened as he released his breath.

"Where you goin', Sunny?" Duke asked him.

Sunny could not believe that Duke had the gall — the audacity, to ask him where he was going. The sarcastic answer was sitting on the tip of his tongue like acid. He was ready to inflict wounds with the words he chose to use even if he was reluctant to lift up his fists to inflict wounds.

"Why the fuck should *you* care where I'm going? I'm just a *'fairy'*, right?"

Duke winced at the words as though they had a presence. A substance that out of the ethereal existence of the spoken word came a power to strike with a physical strength to rival that of a blow by a hand. Duke grabbed Sunny by the arm and started guiding him back to the porch from where he had come. He sought to get Sunny back into his own space from which he could issue forth his words of apology.

"Let's go in da house and talk, bro."

Sunny stopped and caused Duke to stop a well. They were already on the porch. "What's there to talk about, Duke? You just made yourself *perfectly* clear when you were talking to Victorious a few minutes ago."

"It's not like dat," said Duke.

He tried to lead Sunny into the house again and Sunny finally let him guide him in.

"That's not what I meant when I said dat. You know how da game is. You can't look weak or these fools try and test you," Duke said as they walked towards the back of the house.

Sunny didn't reply to Duke until they were in his room. "So I guess you're saying that I'm weak."

"Dat ain't what I'm sayin', man," Duke said. "You know dat, bro. If these fools out here smell blood in da water, dey come swimmin' round like sharks. I can't have dat shit."

"Why should you care what anyone thinks of your sexuality? It doesn't change who you are."

"Yeah, you can say shit like dat for real cause you ain't in the game. It don't matter to you cause you're a civilian, not a soldier."

"Are you serious right now, Duke? You really mean to tell me that you buy into this arbitrary image of what being a man is? What being gay is? Like just because you're out here trappin', you can't love another man? That's bullshit!" Sunny gave in anger. He turned away from Duke, who was sitting on the edge of the bed by now.

"So you telling me that a gay man can't pull the trigger of a gun like a straight man can?" Sunny asked as he turned back to face Duke.

"I ain't gay," Duke said defensively.

Sunny took a step back. He was having difficulties believing what he just heard come out of Duke's mouth. "*What did you say?*" Sunny asked in shock.

"I said '*I ain't gay*', nigga."

"What the fuck do you *think* you are? You think you're not gay just because you're a 'top'?"

"I'm a fuckin' man. I ain't no fag!"

Sunny shook his head in disgust. "So I guess you want to stay in the game too, right?"

"Where else am I gonna cop bands like I got?"

Sunny really could not begin to understand what he was hearing. He refused to say anything further and started to head out of Duke's room. He was disgusted with Duke and disgusted with himself for even being enamored by a man like him. The only thing that he wanted to do right then was just divorce himself from the situation as soon as he possibly could.

Tears welled up in the corners of his eyes and he felt his breath hitch in the beginnings of a sob that he violently squashed down. He absolutely refused to crumble in Duke's presence. He would not cry here.

Duke jumped off of the bed and cut Sunny off before he got to the door of the room. He wrapped Sunny up in his arms and held him close. Everything came crashing down on Sunny as his world seemed to crumble inward. Here was the man that he was starting to love and that man openly denied him in a blatant disregard of his feelings.

It crushed Sunny's heart and his dreams. Crushing his hope for a happy future with Duke. Sunny could not keep the flood waters at bay. As soon as the first tear found a way to fall; found a way to drive down his cheek; found a way to escape, it was over. His fractured self control was finished. He finally gave way to the pain and hurt. He finally let the tears flow freely and the sobs began shortly after that. Sunny was hurt beyond all measure. He drowned in his momentary sorrow.

"I'm sorry, man. I ain't mean none of dat shit. I'm just talkin'. You know what it's like, you gotta be hard or these fools will test you. I ain't mean to hurt chu, bro," said Duke.

Duke kissed Sunny on his neck, his cheek, his lips. He tried to apologize with deeds for the words that had caused the mortal wounds. The words that had drawn blood and left the worst scars ever to be inflicted on him.

Duke's hands caressed. They rubbed, trying to distract, to entice, to ignite a fire that could possibly cause a reversal to what had already transpired. It was an attempt to ameliorate the pain that was caused by his words. His attempts failed. They faltered.

Sunny brushed away the tears. He brushed away the kisses. Sunny brushed away the clinging, hopeful hands so that he could escape from the source of his pain. He wanted and needed to be away and the only way that he was going to get that to happen was to make a break for freedom now, while he still had the strength to do so. If he waited even a second more before he acted on the impetus to leave, then he was going to stay lost and trapped in the cycle of pain that was just beginning to make itself known to him.

Sunny's emotions burned within him like the intense heat of the sun on a scorching summer day. The rift between him and Duke felt like a blinding glare, casting shadows over their connection. The words they'd exchanged were like searing rays, revealing cracks in their foundation. The warmth of their affection had turned into the harsh light of judgment as it burned into ash, and Sunny found himself trapped in the stifling atmosphere of misunderstanding.

SUNNY was able to disentangle himself from Duke long enough to affect an escape from those strong and capable arms. He got in his car and escaped those sensuous lips. That body that made his own body ache with need.

His heart ached. So much so that Sunny soon pulled into the parking lot of a store and stopped his vehicle. He alit from the car and stood at the side of the vehicle taking in great big gasps of air in a bid to keep from sobbing and crying out there in the open, empty parking lot that he had pulled into.

This was not where he wanted to clear out the emotional cobwebs that stuck in the recesses of his mind. Fearful of the daylight that was revealed when the lie was turned aside, Sunny was now able to see the truth about his Adonis; his classical Greek god.

There was hell to pay for having heard the truth of matters from Duke's own lips. To be cast aside, and then denied, hurt worse than he could ever have imagined. What Sunny had left of his hopes and dreams for a future with Duke hung in tatters around the hole in his chest where his heart had once beat so strongly. He was willing to give his heart freely before but now it had been brutally torn from his chest and before he knew it, his heart had been swallowed whole by an ugly beast that he could not run fast enough away from.

Sunny was having trouble coming to grips with how Duke could justify being with a man and then having the gall to consider that he was not gay just because he gave and didn't receive. The tumult in his mind refused to be subdued so that he could make heads or tails of his feelings; of what had actually occurred and what those actions meant for the future.

How was this going to further transform his world, he didn't really know. There was no easy answer. There was no simple solution. Duke had transgressed. The sin of his transgression was monumental. The violation had consequences that might readily, mortally, injure their budding love story in its infancy; while it lay resting peacefully in the crib.

There were things that Sunny was going to have to consider based on the new circumstances. These new changes required a shift in the course of his life as the winds changed and whipped up against his sails. Sunny needed to either furl his sails and wait to see where the prevailing wind would direct him or he was going to have to turn into the wind and tact against it. He was reluctant to turn his stern to the wind and let himself get blown away by the storm. He was not going back to Duke and getting swallowed by that dark storm that was brewing around the man.

Sunny had never run away from a challenge or a fight so he was not going to let the storm blow him away. Sunny was not so desperate to be with someone that he would go immediately back to them after being hurt, so tacking into the wind was definitely out. That left Sunny with only one true option left with which he could chose from and save his fragile soul from further beatings.

He could furl sail and drift in place until the weather patterns ended up giving him a clear indication as to which action he should take to extricate his tender and bleeding heart from the depths of the storm. He would float adrift in the eye of the storm. For now.

The question that begged a speedy answer from him now was what was he to do in this interim period while he was still in shock and trying to process what had happened to his relationship. He had no desire to go back to Duke's place and that obviously didn't need consideration. That was where he was trying to get away from.

He didn't want to go home because he didn't want his father to find out about his heart break. That ultimately led him to the only conclusion possible. That conclusion was for him to go over to Miranda's place and intrude upon her kindness; yet again seek comfort in her gentle presence. She had always been there for him and he was sure that she might again lend her emotional support to him in his time of need. He had no reason to doubt that she would have a cause to turn him away.

Sunny ended up giving Miranda a call on her cell phone. She answered almost immediately and listened patiently as he relayed to her the sum total of events that had just so recently passed between him and Duke. Miranda confessed that at that moment she was not at home but the good news was that he had called and caught her while she was at the grocery store. Miranda told Sunny to meet her at her apartment while she got the essentials that the two of them found necessary when dealing with a heartache or other similar occurrence.

Sunny drove over to Miranda's apartment and waited there for her to return from the grocery store. It didn't take her long to get back to her apartment from the grocery store. They both went inside and settled in front of the television. Miranda had gotten the vanilla ice cream, caramel sauce, graham crackers, and chocolate that was the recipe for their heart ache recovery. Sunny spent the rest of the evening being held and mothered by Miranda as they watched goofy romantic comedies together.

It was exactly the balm that Sunny needed right at that moment to help him begin to recover — at least recover his equilibrium. It was the oasis in the desert that let him escape from the harsh landscape of his turbulent thoughts and emotions. He could take the time to unwind from the stressors and take stock of the many injuries that he had sustained. He could take the time as well to get an accounting of the various causes of those injuries. This was going to be crucial for Sunny in the days to come and Sunny was quick to recognize the importance of taking this time for himself.

Sunny was more grateful that his best friend in the entire world had been able to be there for him when he absolutely needed for her to be there for him the most. Sunny was cognizant of the fact that true friends would always be there for you when you really needed them the most. Miranda was his true friend as far as he was concerned; and always would be.

Amidst of his emotional storm, Sunny found solace in Miranda's presence. She was like a gentle sunbeam breaking through the clouds of his despair. Her kindness and unwavering support acted as a soothing balm for his wounded heart, offering him a respite from a turbulent sea of feelings. As they enjoyed the simple comforts of vanilla ice cream, caramel sauce, and the solace of each other's company, Sunny felt like a sense of safety, shielded from the biting winds of heartache. Miranda's friendship became a steady lantern, guiding him through the darkness, a reminder that even in the midst of agony, moments of warmth and connection could still emerge.

If you called a true friend in the middle of the night and told them that you were in jail, they would not be mad at your plight. They would be mad because you didn't invite them to join into the trouble that got you where you were in the first place. That was the basis of a true friend.

5

Sunny and Miranda spent the rest of the weekend together watching those Rom-Coms and destroying pint after pint of ice cream. Package after package of graham crackers, chocolate, and just as many bottles of caramel sauce.

Sunny was able to push his worries to the side, for the time being, so that he could at least enjoy the time that he was spending with his best friend. He had to change his focus so that he could concentrate on his upcoming gig at the Laugh Factory later on that week. He had Miranda helping him to get the timing right on his delivery and helping him to get his material together so that the flow seemed more natural as he presented it to his audience.

They had eventually retired to Sunny's house. Miranda was sprawled across Sunny's bed. She listened intently to Sunny as he went over his material — again and again. She laughed and giggled and sipped on the beer that she had been nursing since they had begun the rehearsal session. This time spent together was definitely helping Sunny and he was enjoying the rehearsal time as well.

He was enjoying drinking with his friend. He was enjoying spending time with Miranda and not worrying about his relationship with Duke. He was a bit nervous about the upcoming show but that nervousness was overshadowed by the intensity of the excitement of the same upcoming show. Those moments that he would spend in that spot light, being right there in front of that live audience. That feeling was the intoxication that he was seeking.

Miranda was playing around with Sunny while he rehearsed, trying to distract him from being able to give his delivery in the manner that he needed to when he got up on that stage later that evening. He appreciated the attempts because it helped to keep him on his game. This was what he was in need of anyway. Something else to keep his mind from drifting back to his troubled love life. He took playful swipes at Miranda as they continued on.

During all of this, Sunny's phone kept blowing up. The continued buzzing from notifications of missed calls and incoming, unread text messages did act as a distracting force for Sunny as well. The persistent notifications on Sunny's phone were like fleeting shadows that passed in front of the sun, momentarily interrupting his bonding with Miranda.

At each of these notifications, Miranda was drawn to the realization that Sunny's focus was pulled to the phone. That served to throw him off from what he was doing more than Miranda's attempts to do the same.

Sunny was not certain if Miranda was going to let him continue getting away with ignoring his phone without letting her know who it was that was obviously trying to get a hold of him with the continued phone calls and messages. He hoped that she would let it go and just ignore it. Just forget it. Give him a break and let it alone but it was not meant to be and Miranda did eventually clue in on the reason why he avoided the phone and directed her own attention to it.

"Who keeps blowing up your phone, Sunny? Is it your boo? The one that hurt you?"

"I really don't want to talk about it right now. I'd rather we just kept going over my material. Let's do that instead of dealing with the phone," said Sunny tiredly.

He was trying to get away from having to face the realization of what was going on in his life with Duke. He wanted to try to put it out of his mind for as long as he could. He wanted to believe that things were okay — at least for now. Just these few minutes. He just wanted the peace, at least for another few minutes.

"Every time that phone blows up, you throw your timing," Miranda scolded.

"It's not like that."

"You're trying to lie to me about it and I'm right here looking at you. I know you, Sunny. We've been close for too many years now for you to be able to bullshit me. I can tell that this drama is still bugging the hell outta you right now."

Sunny sighed. His shoulders dropped and he slowly sank down on his bed beside Miranda. "I don't know what I should do Miranda. I really liked him and he hurt me bad."

"I can understand that," she consoled.

When Sunny had gone over to Miranda's house after leaving from Duke's place. She had asked for no specifics about why she needed to be there for her best friend. The need was there and that was all that she required from Sunny so that she could be there for *him*. The need was there and at that time the pain that Sunny was suffering poured off of him in sheets. Miranda had asked for no explanation and at that time, Sunny had given nothing to Miranda in the way of a full explanation for why he was in need of her support as his friend.

Sunny told her that things had turned bad with Duke but that was about all that he said. Miranda had patiently spent time with Sunny on that night. That was then though; that was when just being there for Sunny was the most important thing in the world. That moment was definitely in the past and the present moment was now fully upon them and things were different.

"So do you feel like talking about it now? It's been a few days since it all happened."

"I don't know if I'm ready to deal with it yet," said Sunny slowly while drawing the words out slowly and fiddling with his own fingers..

Sunny started staring at his folded hands that he had sitting in his lap.

"You're going to have to deal with it sooner or later, dude. It might as well be *now* instead of *later*. I'm here for you," said Miranda.

"I know. I know you are," Sunny whispered. He looked over at Miranda and smiled at her. She smiled back and patted Sunny on the knee.

Sunny was sitting on the side of the bed and Miranda had been laying on it on her belly so that she could face Sunny when he was standing before her earlier and he was practicing. She now had flipped around so that she could kick her legs off of the bed and sit up next to Sunny. When she was upright, she wrapped her arms around Sunny and drew him backwards so that they both fell to a lying position on the bed. Both of them laughed because of Miranda's antics.

"So spill the beans already, you bum. Let me know what's going on in your life between you and your bae. What really happened that night?" asked Miranda.

Sunny was not sure if he was ready to tell Miranda what had really happened. He was not sure he was ready to deal with what had happened himself, but maybe — just maybe, Miranda would be able to help him work through everything that had happened between him and Duke. Maybe Miranda might just be the one to give him insight into his conflicted feelings about Duke and what Duke had said and done.

"I'm not sure that he's the one anymore. I'd love for him to be my bae but I don't think that it'll work out," said Sunny.

He threw his hands behind his head while Miranda moved into a position where she would be able to stretch out across Sunny. Miranda ended up laying perpendicular to Sunny. She rested her head on his broad chest and stared at him. Sunny's head was propped up enough on a pillow, and his hands, that he afforded Miranda the ability to see his solemn face.

"So what happened exactly then? I mean you were telling me that he was the one for you not too long ago and now you're not so sure?"

"Something like that. I came up on him and your man Victorious was there talking to him."

"What?" exclaimed Miranda in surprise. "You met Black Vic?"

"Yeah. He and Duke —,"

"Duke?" interrupted Miranda in surprise. "Are you talking about Anthony Williams? *That* 'Duke'?"

Sunny was irked because he had let the name of the guy he was seeing slip out when he hadn't meant to. He had wanted to keep that information to himself until he was certain that the relationship was going to work out or not. Just thinking about it now made him almost tear up.

"Yeah, it's Anthony."

"I didn't know he was gay."

"*He* didn't know either," Sunny said sarcastically. His dry humor coming from the anger and frustration he felt at remembering the incident.

"What's that supposed to mean?" Miranda asked. She wasn't sure where Sunny's anger was coming from and the reasoning behind his comment.

"When Black Vic confronted him about being with me, Duke got defensive and denied being gay right in front of me — well...I was on the porch of his house listening but, it was a bunch of bullshit if you ask me!"

"So you are telling me that the biggest gas mover on the south side of ATL is actually gay?"

"Yes," Sunny revealed with a breath of air escaping his lips.

Miranda was shocked but tried not to show it. She asked, "why didn't you tell me that he was the one that you were with?"

"First off, I didn't know that you knew Duke like that. Second off, I wasn't sure if it was going to work out so I kept it to myself. I was going to let you know about it if it had actually worked out between us. I just wanted to be certain. Is that so bad of a thing?"

"No, you're right," said Miranda. "I guess it was smart to try and wait. I can't believe that he lied about being gay, though."

"Yeah, it hurt bad when I heard what he said about being gay."

Miranda stared at Sunny. He tried hard to hide the hurt but he could not disguise the impact of the hurt showing upon his face. He could not stop it from reflecting in his eyes. Sunny was of the opinion that Miranda could easily read his emotions. She was the closest friend that he had on the planet and they had been through a lot together after all.

It would have been easy for her to read those hidden emotions and that was the thing that brought them closer to each other. There was that bond. There was that intertwined emotional connection that bound them closer together than if they had even shared the same blood and were actual brother and sister. They were close enough as they were. There was no need to be even closer. They were close enough to give the other the love and support that the other needed and that was no matter what happened between them.

After an indeterminate amount of time, in which Miranda had continued her survey of Sunny, she made up her mind to speak again. It was just a quick thought that she voiced before she thought better of it. "If we were really tight, you would have told me about Duke whether or not it was gonna work out with you guys."

Sunny peeked down at Miranda. "We are tight. You're the closest thing to a sister that I have."

Miranda said nothing. She continued staring at Sunny with a sullen look on her face. Sunny was not sure what was on Miranda's mind. He had never seen her act like that towards him before. It was so out of the ordinary and out of character for Miranda. It was so far away from the Miranda that he knew — the Miranda that he had grown up with. The Miranda that he loved so dearly and cherished so much.

For all of the pain and hurt that Sunny was feeling — that he was going through, at that moment in time, it seemed to him that there was an issue that was troubling Miranda as well. He began to wonder about her conflict. He pushed aside all of his own baggage for a moment that was long enough for him to recognize something that he had never recognized in his friend before.

There was a deeply buried pain that shimmered just below the thin surface emotions that she just so happened to show the world. There was something there, right now, in the way that she looked into his face. Something in the glint of her eyes that told him of its singular presence.

Miranda tried to look away but Sunny was too quick for her. He sandwiched her face between his hands and held her gaze steadily with his own. He searched, but could not find what it was that he was looking to find so deeply in her eyes. A second ago, what he was looking for in her eyes to find, was right there for him to recognize and comprehend. Now, however, it was no where to be found and Sunny was just as perplexed now as he had been when he thought that there had indeed been something to find.

What had been there? What exactly was it that he had seen that had given him pause enough to cast his own worries away in order to take hers deftly upon his shoulders. To carry the weight of her worries like Atlas holding the earth up in the heavens. What had called out to him like a light in the gloomy night. Whatever it had been, it was gone now and hadn't even had the decency to leave a shadow of its existence for Sunny to find.

Miranda's eyes now brimmed with tears of her own. She jerked her head to the side and Sunny's hands fell away. She buried her face in Sunny's chest. Her emotions surged like the sun's brilliance, momentarily blinding him with their intensity. "Why couldn't you tell me? You don't trust me enough to know, is that it?"

"It's not like that, Miranda," pled Sunny plaintively.

"Then what's it like? Really? I want to know. We've been close for too long for you to turn around and hold something like this out on me. I really wanna know why," cried Miranda.

"I'm not really sure. I mean I've always told you about any guys I've been with but this time things were just...I don't know...different. I was looking for a long term relationship and I guess I was just too focused on that to pay attention to those people that were around me."

"I don't like seeing you hurt, Sunny," declared Miranda.

"I appreciate that, Miranda, but that's not really your job to keep me from getting hurt. We're supposed to support one another when we do get hurt because we're friends."

"But I love you, Sunny. I don't ever want to see you get hurt."

"I love you too, Miranda," said Sunny in response to the plaintive tone in Miranda's voice.

"No, you idiot," Miranda said suddenly. "I *love* you."

Miranda crawled up towards Sunny so that she was face to face with him. She hung over him — close, but not touching. Sunny could see her nostrils flair and the smooth dark skin of her lovely face. He could feel the gentleness of her breath against his cheek and his lips. Her own lips trembled just slightly before she fell down on him in a deep and a passionate kiss. Sunny was shocked. He was so shocked by what was happening at the moment between him and Miranda that at first, he did nothing. He didn't respond.

It was only after Miranda had shifted her body so that she could stretch out and lay atop him that he even dared to move at all. His hands moved slowly to Miranda's waist and he carefully applied just enough of his strength to cause the two of them to separate in a hot exchange of breath.

"What was that, Miranda," gasped Sunny in surprise. He was still too shocked by what had just transpired to really give a single straight thought to the action. She had severely thrown him off. He was dazed and confused beyond belief.

"What the hell?" Sunny asked again with his face twisted in bewilderment, shock, and wonder.

"I...I," stammered Miranda. She recoiled in fear in the face of the rejection that Sunny had just displayed. "I love you," she whispered finally.

Sunny was still in shock and so he was not really cognizant of the impact of his actions and the words he chose to use right then. He gave no indication that he understood that what he did right then might have more of an impact than he knew because of the vulnerable spot that Miranda had placed herself in.

He was not understanding that his best friend had opened herself up completely to him. She had made of herself a vulnerable and fragile thing like a flower. Like a sunflower blowing on the breeze.

Sunny had a flustered look on his face. His thoughts were muddled when he said, "I'm gay, Miranda. You know that."

Sunny would not have thought to say those words to Miranda had what had just passed between them been an innocent thing. If it had been an innocent kiss. That had been no innocent kiss. There had been too much tenderness there, coupled with the eroticism that had been implied, for it to be considered anywhere near an innocent kiss. What that kiss had done was to leave astonishment, incertitude, and anger in its wake.

Miranda sat upright on the bed and refused to face Sunny. Sunny came upright on the bed beside Miranda and for a few minutes. The both of them were seated there. They were near enough to one another to touch, if they dared to, but neither did.

Neither one of the two of them reached out to have that physical connection with the other. Neither one of them was inclined to do so after dealing with that last bit of intimate, physical contact. It was still too fresh and raw in their minds; burning on their lips. The after math was still just crumbling down around them.

Sunny finally found some words to speak after working his mouth open and closed looking to say *something* — *anything,* to fill the void. "We've known each other since middle school, Miranda. In all of that time, you've known I was gay. Nothing has changed that between then and now."

Sunny thought that Miranda would say something in response; that she would offer up something to explain what had happened. Maybe she would issue an apology for her most recent actions. Nothing like that happened. Instead, Miranda scooted down to the edge of the bed where she could stand up.

Miranda slowly gathered her things together without looking back at Sunny. She refused to even acknowledge his presence even once during that time. Sunny watched as she gathered her things together and left his bedroom.

Sunny could have reached out to stop her from leaving — but he didn't. Sunny could have said something to stop her from leaving — but he didn't. He let her slowly slip away and with her leaving, she took a piece of Sunny's heart with her. Miranda was crying freely as she walked out of the door to Sunny's bedroom and Sunny could tell. Still, he did nothing to slow her down and stop her from leaving his presence.

Sunny stood up and followed her out as she left the room. He had every intention in the world of just calling out to her retreating back. He had his hand raised as if he would catch hold of Miranda and draw her back to him but he hesitated. He stalled out as Miranda pushed past his father, Peter and went to leave the house.

Sunny failed to stop Miranda from leaving because he was brought up short by the look of disappointment that had just appeared on his father's pale face. His father had looked at Miranda as she had slipped past him. He had gotten a gist of what may have occurred between the two of them. That Sunny had hurt her severely was easy for him to see, but *how* Sunny had hurt her — he didn't know. He realized that something major had gone on between the two of them and Sunny had ended up hurting her enough that she ran away from him.

Sunny finally gathered the courage to chase after her. He caught her in the driveway. His heart raced as he remembered watching Miranda gather her belongings, her movements were a portrait of sadness and anger. He stood there, a mixture of regret and confusion churning within him. "Miranda, wait," he finally managed to utter, his voice barely above a whisper.

Miranda paused but didn't turn around, her body tense. "What do you want to say *now*, Sunny?"

Her words were tinged with a bitterness that cut through him.

Sunny hesitated, the weight of his emotions pressing down on him. "I never meant for things to turn out like this. I didn't expect any of it," he began, his voice shaking. "But I should have told you about Duke, I should've been honest with you from the start."

Miranda turned to face him, her eyes red and swollen from tears. "Honestly? After all these years, do you really think that's all I wanted? You were my *best friend*, Sunny. I thought we shared everything, but it feels like you shut me out when it mattered the most."

Sunny's heart ached as he listened to her words. "I never wanted to hurt you, Miranda. I was scared, confused, and I thought I could handle my feelings on my own."

Miranda let out a bitter laugh, her anger mixing with sadness. "You think this is about you being *gay*, Sunny? It's not. It's about *you* not trusting *me* enough to share your struggles. I would have been here for you, no matter what."

Tears welled up in Sunny's eyes as he reached out toward her, his hand trembling. "Miranda, I've known you for so long, and I've always cared about you. I never imagined that my own confusion would end up hurting you like this."

Miranda's gaze softened slightly, but her pain was still evident. "I *know* you care, Sunny. But it's not just about caring; it's about understanding and communication. We're supposed to be a team, facing life's challenges together."

Sunny's shoulders slumped, the weight of his mistakes almost suffocating him. "I messed up, Miranda. I messed up so badly, and I don't know how to make things right."

Miranda's expression softened further, and she took a step closer to him. "You're right, you messed up. But we can't change the past. What we can do is decide what our friendship means to us now."

As the emotional roller coaster swept through their lives, the immediate repercussions of Miranda's earlier actions remained unaddressed and temporarily relegated to oblivion. The significance of the kiss and its implications were placed on the back burner. Sunny, instead of delving into the aftermath of that intimate moment, was preoccupied with her feelings of hurt. He grappled with the fact that he hadn't opened up to Miranda, hindering the recollection of his genuine response and justifiable anger towards her impulsive initiative to kiss him.

Sunny looked into her eyes, the depth of his regret and longing mirrored in his gaze. "I want to make things right, Miranda. I want to earn back your trust. We had always promised to tell each other everything."

Miranda's features softened, a glimmer of hope shining through. "If you had told me about Duke in the first place, I might have been able to warn you about that jackass. It won't be easy, Sunny. Rebuilding trust takes time. But if you're willing to be open with me, to let me in, we can start working through this together."

Sunny nodded, a mixture of determination and vulnerability in his eyes. "I want to try, Miranda. I want us to be more than just friends again."

Miranda's lips twitched in a small smile. "We have a long way to go, Sunny. But if you're willing to put in the effort, then maybe, just maybe, we can find a way to heal and move forward."

As they stood there, facing each other with a world of emotions between them, Sunny knew that the journey ahead wouldn't be easy.

But he was ready to confront his mistakes, to learn from them, and to fight for the bond he had with Miranda—the bond that had weathered so much, but had the potential to emerge even stronger.

Sunny's phone buzzed, pulling him out of his reverie. He picked it up, surprised to see Duke's name on the caller ID. The complications in his life were multiplying, and he realized he was at a crossroads. He had a choice to make—between facing his past mistakes and pursuing a chance at happiness with Miranda, or exploring the potential of a renewed relationship with Duke, fraught with uncertainties and challenges. As he looked at the phone in his hand, Sunny knew that whatever path he chose, it would shape his future and define the relationships that meant the most to him.

SUNNY stood with his hands posted on the back of his head. Eventually his hands slowly lowered to his side and Miranda disappeared from his view. His mind retraced its steps to that lingering kiss and the earnest words Miranda had shared about the importance of transparency in their relationship. It dawned on him that, in return, she had been concealing significant aspects from him—important revelations left unspoken.

As he replayed the incident in his thoughts, it became apparent that she had employed her own anger as a shield, deflecting the need to confront the very issues she had accused him of. The realization hit him: she, too, hadn't been entirely forthcoming. The more he dwelled on it, the more his frustration mounted at the realization that she had deftly manipulated the situation, preventing him from addressing her for actions she mirrored from his own.

He turned from the driveway and went towards the front of the house so that she could leave without him chasing behind her. The look of disappointment on his father's face only served to cause Sunny to suddenly shift to a defensive posture. His fists slowly curled up and he crossed his arms in front of his chest to keep from doing something rash that he would later regret.

Sunny's field of vision narrowed on the man that stood before him in the doorway. He knew that it was too late to catch up with Miranda before she left so he just let her go. He let her fade away out of his mind so that the anger flooding over him, because of his father's disapproving look, would have room to grow. He felt like taking his raw emotions out on somebody and his father was right there, judging him, as Sunny felt he always did.

"What?" fired Sunny belligerently; rudely.

Peter let the disrespectful manner and attitude wash over him and he ignored it; he completely disregarded it even.

"You're an ass, son," said Peter as he turned and started walking into the house. He stopped when Sunny ended up replying to him.

"And what's that supposed to mean?" Sunny demanded, suddenly shocked that his father had called him an ass.

The anger seemed to evaporate from Sunny. Peter turned around. Sunny faced his father. Peter had never said one cross word to Sunny that he would have ever considered as verbal abuse until right then.

"It means that you've been friends with that girl for over ten years and you don't know the first damn thing about her," Peter said softly.

"I know her —," began Sunny.

"You don't know *shit*, boy. That girl has loved you since the day that you two met. Hell, I saw it in her eyes when you first brought her home."

Peter walked away from his son and into the house. He was heading to his own bedroom in the rear of the house. He stopped at his bedroom door and stood with his hand laying lightly on the doorknob. He hoped that the sun would break through the clouds of their misunderstanding.

His back saw still to his son as he spoke again. "If she's really important to you, Sunny, you should do everything in your power to make sure that she's okay right now. Losing someone who loves you unconditionally feels like you've lost a part of who you are. If you're not careful, you'll let that loss destroy you in the end."

Peter turned the doorknob, opened the door, and disappeared into the interior of his bedroom. He closed the door swiftly behind himself and left Sunny out in the hallway, lost in the myriad of thoughts that now ran rampant through his head. He could not figure out if his father was talking about him losing Miranda or his father losing his mother.

Sunny didn't think that it was fair. Miranda was just as much in the wrong as he was. Things in his life had just gotten so complicated and there was nothing that he could do about it. There was also, now, a lack of someone that he could share this with that would be able to help him deal with the complexities. Help him figure out what the hell he had missed in all of this.

There things stood and Sunny came to the realization that the events in his life right then were getting way beyond his own ability to deal with. His anchor had just left out of the front door of his house and things were knotty now between them; he had no idea how he was going to fix these things. He was having a hard time just trying to figure out if what problems he was currently facing were problems of his own making or the result of others.

Sunny walked back to his bedroom. He flopped down on the bed and then he released a deep breath. He closed his eyes so that he could think about what had happened. Dwell on the feelings that were now so obvious from Miranda. He had to figure out where he was going now and how he was supposed to get there. Only then would he be able to understand what he had to do when he finally did get there.

Sunny laid down on his bed. He rolled over until he was laying on his belly. He buried his face into his pillow and let out a muffled scream of his pent up frustrations. He felt like his problems were supposed to have been getting better but instead, his problems, and therefore his life, were getting more convoluted and far from being anything near to easy. What was he to do? He didn't know in the slightest.

Sunny's phone buzzed, letting him know that he had an incoming call from someone. Sunny jumped up quickly to answer the phone sitting on his nightstand. He thought that maybe Miranda was reaching out and calling him. Maybe they just might be able to work out what had happened between them. Fix it. Make things right. Then they would be able to move on like before. Before all of — this. Before.

Sunny connected with the caller before he took the time to verify who was actually calling him. If he had just taken the time to check his caller identification, then the voice that he heard, that answered his, would have had less power to give him a shock.

"Hey, bro," said Duke. "I been tryna' get a hold of you for a while, yo. What's good?"

"Duke?" queried Sunny confusedly.

"Yeah, man. It's me. I just wanted to holla at chu for a minute and let chu know I was sorry about how all dat went down. You doin' aight?"

Sunny was not sure how much of his current emotional state he wanted Duke to be aware of. There was so much that was going on for him to truly keep up with. Duke was just serving to add more complications to the mix. On top of it all, he was still into Duke. He was still into him in a big way that didn't seem to want to diminish by the least little bit given the small amount of time that had passed.

"I'm alright, Duke. Things...are just a little complicated for me right now," said Sunny.

Duke sighed. "Look, man. I gotta apologize, dude. I was on dat gas and I was talkin' dat fuck shit. I don't mean nonna dat shit. I was talkin' outta the side of my neck on the for real. I'm tryna' keep it real with chu and be wit' chu."

"Duke, how am I supposed to feel when you can't even admit that you're gay? Are we going to be a couple? Is it always going to be a thing where I'm your dirty little secret? I can't be in a relationship like that. It's not fair to me and it's not what I want in my life."

"I know, man. You right. Dat shit ain't fair and I'm ready to let the world know 'bout us. I can't keep you a secret no mo."

Sunny was surprised to hear that. "Are you serious? I mean, are you really sure that's what you want?"

"I want chu, Sunny. I'll do what I gotta do to keep you comin' round so come on back. Let's do dis thang."

"I don't know, Duke. You really hurt me."

"I promise you I won't do dat shit no mo. I got chu, brah."

"Okay, Duke. Let's take it slow for right now. We'll see where this thing goes," said Sunny.

Duke's excitement was palpable. It was infectious and Sunny felt himself warming up just a little, despite the trouble that was going on with Miranda; and his reservations about Duke.

6

As the sun cast it's golden rays upon the city, Black Vic rolled down the window on the passenger side of the car that he was riding in so that he could gawk at the pretty girls walking up and down the street next to the West End Mall in Atlanta. Two of his goons were in the car with him. These were his main shooters and they were rarely seen without Black Vic. These were the same two individuals that had originally pulled up on Duke and Sunny as they were leaving the park after they had finished playing basketball.

The guy that was driving the car went by the name of Echo and the young kid that was sitting in the passenger side, behind Black Vic, was called Bingo. Black Vic took a tote on a blunt that he had gotten from Bingo. He took a second, deep drag, and passed the blunt on to the driver of the car, Echo.

Black Vic leaned back in the seat and issued forth a billowing cloud of smoke that he had just taken down into his lungs. He took a sip of the malt liquor that he had just recently purchased and he watched as the world unfolded around him.

People walking back and forth in the early evening hour. Lights flashing and pulsing all around him, adding to the calming effects of the marijuana and the lethargic feeling that was advanced by the consumption of the beer. He looked over at Echo and watched as the driver delivered his own addition to the smoke that filled the interior of the car.

"Yo, Echo," said Black Vic.

"Yeah," Echo answered.

"Chu know who Duke is, right?"

"Yeah. Me and Bingo ran into 'em at the park over on Lakewood Ave da other day. Him and some dude was dere ballin'. Why you ask, yo?"

Black Vic smiled wickedly. "What did the dude wit' Duke look like? Did chu peep 'em?"

"Yeah, man. He was some old yella nigga. He play a hustle on da b-ball at some of da local courts."

"For real?" asked Black Vic.

When Echo confirmed that with a nod, Black Vic started talking again. "That yella nigga is a fairy," said Black Vic.

Bingo chimed into the conversation from the backseat. "You serious? Do Duke know he kickin' it wit' a flammer?"

"Duke knows. I called 'em out on it. I think he suckin' on dat high yella meat pipe," said Black Vic.

"So dat nigga's bitch made?" asked Echo.

"From what I seen, dat nigga need to be wearing a dress and some pumps," Black Vic declared.

All three of the guys started laughing uproariously. It seemed that they found more than a little humor in making fun of Duke. Black Vic kept adding fuel to the fire. "Dat bitch made nigga prob'ly takin' it up da ass. I knew he was a fuckin' pussy."

"Word, man. Dat pussy think he own da south side and got it locked. I say we hit dat fool and burn out dat trap house he runnin' over on Gammon," said Echo.

Black Vic took a hit of the blunt again and passed it back to the back of the car for Bingo to take a hit. "Ya think dey got some gas and band-o's dere?"

"My man say dey cop bout ten to twenty bags a time there. Dey s'pose to be countin' that bread there too, ya heard?" said Bingo.

Black Vic looked over at Echo. "How many you need?"

"Shooters?" asked Echo.

"Yeah," said Black Vic.

"Me and Bingo can take dat by ourselves. No cap."

"How many ops chu think posted up in dere?" asked Black Vic.

Bingo did the mental math in his head and then said, "My man told me dat da house be packed wit' dem smokers and dey got one young blood dere all da time, passin' out dem zannie's and da gas and takin' dat paper, ya heard?"

Black Vic sat in silence for a long while before he said anything else. The blunt made another pass in rotation before Black Vic flicked it out of the window without hesitation. He pulled out his cell phone and sent a text message out to Miranda. Upon her prompt reply, Black Vic had Echo change directions so that he could be dropped off at her apartment.

"I want chu and Bingo to go 'head and take care a dat," Black Vic directed.

Echo nodded and kept the car moving towards their destination. When Echo got them outside of Miranda's apartment, he stopped the car and regarded Black Vic.

"How long you think its gonna take you to shake dat down?" Black Vic asked Echo.

Echo hummed and drummed his fingers on the steering wheel of the car while he did a mental estimation of the time that it would take him and Bingo to rob the trap house that Duke controlled.

"I got da poles for bof us already and we got dem masks so we ain't gotta stop and get none of dat. We can take it down in 'bout twenty minutes. It'll take 'bout twenty minutes to get dere from here so we should be back here in 'bout an hour, maybe," said Echo.

Black Vic agreed and gave Echo and Bingo some dap before he got out of the car. He let them go so that they could go and take care of business at the trap house. He left to go and meet up with Miranda in her apartment. Black Vic's shooters understood what was expected of them and he had no doubt at all that they would be up to the task of taking down the trap house. He wanted the drugs. He wanted the money that was likely to be there as well.

Most of all, Black Vic wanted to deal a blow to Duke that would hurt his operation and serve to possibly bring Duke down a peg or two in his eyes. He wanted Duke to hurt a little and he was willing to do whatever it was going to take to make that happen. He didn't like the fact that Duke pressed him outside of his home. In his mind, it was disrespectful.

Black Vic got to the front door of the apartment and he rang the doorbell to announce his presence to Miranda. When she failed to answer the door fast enough, he took to giving the door a few good, hard raps to try and get Miranda to speed up and get the front door opened so that he could make his way into her apartment.

Miranda answered the door in a state of undress. Black Vic was fine with that, he didn't mind how she was dressed in the least. That was because it was his intent to try and get her naked as soon as he possibly could so that he could have sex with her.

Miranda was wearing a towel wrapped snuggly around her body and her hair was dripping wet. It was apparent that she had just quit the shower so that she could attend to the incessant knocking at her front door. She saw Black Vic standing in her doorway. She hurriedly ushered him into the apartment so that she could go ahead and close the outside world off again. When she noted that it was Black Vic standing at her threshold, demanding entrance, she gave up on the idea of getting back into the shower. She had gotten the time to wash her body but Black Vic had arrived prior to her being able to wash her hair.

Black Vic waved his boys off as Miranda closed the door. When he was certain that the door was locked, he swept Miranda up into his arms. Miranda let out a 'whoop' in surprise, just before Black Vic locked and fixed his lips upon hers and gave her a passionate kiss.

His tongue slipped between her lips and she found herself immediately in a French kiss that lasted some few minutes before Black

Vic at last released her from the kiss. This allowed them both the few minutes necessary to catch their collective breaths.

Black Vic didn't waste much more time. He deftly relieved Miranda of her towel, using one hand in a quick and sure maneuver. The towel fell from her body and pooled on the floor at her feet. It would end up being ignored for the rest of the time that they spent together; Black Vic and Miranda both. Their grasping hands sought purchase upon flesh that was heated from excitement and pending passionate concourse. Inhibitions fell away as the towel had fallen away from Miranda's body, leaving her exposed. Her nudity open to the space that the two of them occupied.

Black Vic's hand entangled itself into Miranda's hair and he pulled down hard enough to have her break their kiss as her head snapped backwards and caused her to emit an audible gasp. He attacked her neck. Black Vic bit her. He attacked, attached and sucked on her neck with enough pressure to leave a bruise upon the tender skin.

Miranda was aroused to the point of distraction. Her nipples stood erect on her high, perky breasts. He took one of those nipples into his mouth, sure and firm. He worked it with his tongue and then bit the tender flesh, causing Miranda to gasp again with her new intake of breath. A gasp of pleasure and pain combined.

Black Vic spun the petite girl around in his arms until her back rested firmly upon his chest. One hand was gripped cruelly on her upper left arm while the right hand crept down the dark skin of her belly. Moisture covered her body and it was hard to tell at that point if that moisture was from the aborted shower that she had earlier left from, or if it was from the heat created by their mutual, carnal passions. In that moment, it mattered little.

The broad hand, with its rough fingers, passed the border of her waist and the fingers trespassed into the valley between her legs. The fingers played with the soft silky hairs before moving on to find a nubbin in which ultra sensitive nerves dwelled. That nexus became the object at the center stage that served to draw the attention of both Miranda and then Black Vic. The spotlight was focused there, for the moment.

He refused to leave that place alone until Miranda's knees weakened and her body began to shake with the first of the many orgasms that Black Vic would eventually bring her to. The point of her lasciviousness was just right there at the periphery of her arousal. It took very little to send her tumbling headlong across that divide and into the yawning mass of ecstasy that awaited her just inside of that zone. Black Vic held Miranda up with that one, crudely grasping hand as the other hand worked her over even more, to bring her to the brink of her second orgasm. Black Vic let her tumble to the floor this time. He didn't choose to help her steady herself as her knees began to weaken and her legs began to buckled beneath her.

Black Vic stared at his fingers. They were slick with Miranda's dew; yet another sign of how turned on Miranda was. Black Vic loved her excitement. It fed and drove the beast within him. Miranda was seated on her thighs in her position on the floor. Her hands supported her and kept her from falling down as she took ragged breaths.

Miranda's head hung low and her legs were folded beneath her. Black Vic took her face into his hand and placed the wet fingers of his right hand into her open lips when she was eventually turned to face him. Miranda's lips parted readily, just as her other lips had parted for the same fingers just moments before. Her slippery tongue snaked out of her mouth and between Black Vic's slightly spread fingers. He worked his fingers in and out of her mouth rhythmically. She surrendered herself completely to the actions being forced on her.

"Chu ready for dis dick, bitch," asked Black Vic as he began to unfasten his pants with his free hand.

Black Vic didn't give Miranda much in the way of an option to try and respond to his question. He kept his fingers in her open and hot mouth and his fingers played with Miranda's tongue. Black Vic eventually recovered his fingers from Miranda's mouth so that he could replace it with his engorged member. She took the length of Black Vic into her mouth and slowly began to give him oral pleasure. It was a prelude to other acts of sex that they would end up engaging in later on in the evening.

Miranda pleasured herself as she continued to give fellatio to Black Vic. Her fingers brought her to yet another shuddering release. Black Vic watched Miranda as her fingers worked in her sex. He allowed her to continue as she was doing for another ten minutes before he stopped her and had her stand up from her kneeling position.

Black Vic led Miranda over to the couch where he sat down. He had Miranda straddle his lap where she was facing him. They were joined together intimately when she lowered herself into his waiting lap. Miranda leaned forward until she was in a position where she could comfortably lock lips with Black Vic.

Black Vic allowed the kiss that he got from Miranda to continue on for a short time and then he pushed Miranda away and leaned back on the couch. He took that position so that he could watch Miranda as she worked her hips back and forth in her efforts to bring them both to their climax. Black Vic spread his arms along the back of the couch and he gave a smile while he watched Miranda work.

Miranda placed her hands behind her, on Black Vic's knees. This gave her the position that she needed to get the leverage that she wanted. This position placed him inside of her at the right spot. As she got further into her ardor, she threw her head back and began vocalizing from deep within as she drew each of her raspy breaths. She began to pant as she continued to work, until eventually, Black Vic leaned forward and tied Miranda up in the embrace of his arms. He was close to his own climax and within a few moments, it was upon him. He released his seed inside of Miranda just as she, herself, began to orgasm due to Black Vic's increase in movement. The friction hitting the right place.

Miranda collapsed into Black Vic's arms and rested her head on his shoulder. Her breath, like his, came in ragged gulps as they both sought to recover from their strenuous exertions of a second ago. Eventually, Black Vic leaned back and pushed Miranda off of his lap, with little regard for her wanting to move off of him or not. Black Vic adjusted himself and used the towel, that Miranda was previously wrapped in, to clean himself off. When he was done, he tossed the towel over to Miranda, put himself back together, and sat back down on the couch beside her.

"Damn, girl," he said absently to Miranda.

Miranda wrapped the towel back around her body and just sat there regarding Black Vic. Black Vic pulled a pack of cigarettes out of his pocket and was just about to remove one of them from the pack. He would have done just that — and lit it up, but Miranda spoke against him doing so.

"Don't light that in here, Black Vic," Miranda said.

Black Vic looked over at Miranda, in mid motion of getting ready to smoke the cigarette.

"Chu bugging, girl." Black Vic laughed and popped the unlit cigarette into his mouth and began fishing in his pocket for a lighter.

Miranda leaned over and pulled the unlit cigarette out of Black Vic's mouth before he could light it with the lighter that he had finally fished out of his pocket and now held cupped between his hands. She placed the unlit cigarette on the coffee table in front of them. "I'm serious, Black Vic. You can go out on the balcony and smoke but I don't want you smoking in my apartment."

The muscles along Black Vic's jaw had tensed up momentarily and he had clenched his fists. His automatic reaction to Miranda taking his cigarette had caused him to narrow his eyes at her in anger but he quickly took a calming breath, let it out slowly and leaned back into the cushions of the couch.

Black Vic turned away from her and looked at his cigarette on the coffee table and said casually, "I saw yo man's da otha' day."

"Who?" Miranda asked curiously.

Her forehead was wrinkled up in concentration, trying to guess who Black Vic might be talking about.

"Who are you talking about?" she asked again as she watched Black Vic pick up the discarded cigarette in his hand.

Black Vic chuckled, "Chu know. Da fairy." He completed saying while he held his hand out and let his wrist droop until his fingers were pointed downwards.

"You met Sunny?" Miranda asked surprised.

"Yea. Dat's da fairy's name."

"He is not a fairy. He is my friend. His name is Sunny," said Miranda testily.

Her thoughts retraced the path to the shared kiss with Sunny, the ripples of which lingered in the aftermath. A sense of guilt washed over her as she acknowledged the manipulation that had colored their argument, preventing Sunny from addressing the incident. She recognized her wrongdoing, understanding that she had initially withheld information from him. Notably, she had concealed her feelings for Sunny far longer than he had kept his secret about Duke. The weight of her actions bore heavily on her conscience, and she grappled with the idea that self-forgiveness might prove elusive in the face of what she had done.

Miranda wrapped the towel tighter around her body and arranged it so that it would not fall off of her. She got up, went into the kitchen and opened the refrigerator so that she could get a beer. She came back out of the kitchen and walked past Black Vic. On her way past him, she took the cigarette from Black Vic's fingers. She took the lighter from his other hand and she moved to the balcony door, opened it up, and stepped outside.

Miranda struck the lighter to the cigarette, causing it to fire up. She inhaled deeply. She didn't normally like smoking but Black Vic had gotten on her nerves. The sex with him was great but talking to him was frustrating. She felt like she needed the cigarette break from Black Vic. Black Vic came out onto the balcony behind Miranda and slipped the beer from her unresisting grip and took a swig. They exchanged items afterwards; Black Vic gave her the beer back and she passed him the cigarette.

"I seent Sunny over at Duke's place," said Black Vic.

Miranda sighed. She leaned on the railing of the balcony and looked out into the night. Cars passed by on the street outside of the fenced in parking lot. It was a pretty evening and the temperature was mild enough that Miranda was not uncomfortable being outside dressed in only the towel.

"Sunny likes Duke and they're supposed to be kicking it together," said Miranda absently before she realized what she had just said.

She was not sure if Sunny had wanted that information known to the public yet if he had kept it from her as well as everyone else in the world.

"Chu jokin', right?" Black Vic asked.

Miranda turned and faced Black Vic. She had a look on her face indicating the disappointment that she felt towards herself for letting that information slip from her lips.

"Let it go, Black Vic. I don't think Sunny wanted anyone to know about that yet. I mean, he even kept it a secret from *me* and the only reason I know is because he let it slip out."

Miranda wore a pout, her thoughts in disarray. The inadvertent disclosure of her own secret to Sunny left her in turmoil. Now, she grappled with the distraction spawned by the revelations she never meant to share—confidential details about her best friend now known to someone unintended. There was a concern what Black Vic would do with this information but there was little that she could do about it now.

Black Vic let out a hearty laugh. He held up his hands in front of himself in mock defense from Miranda's chastisement. "Woah. Cool. I ain't heard nuthin'. I'll let it go."

Miranda eyed Black Vic speculatively and took the beer back from him. "You better," she said as she took another sip and looked back out over the traffic beyond and below her.

A car horn sounded from the parking lot below them. Miranda looked down and saw a young black man standing beside the driver's door of a dark, four door sedan with dark tint.

"Isn't that Echo down there?" Miranda asked, pointing out the individual to Black Vic.

Black Vic looked down and smiled when he recognized Echo.

"Yeah, dat's Echo. Dat's my ride," he said as he turned and patted Miranda on the ass. "I got shit to go take care of. I'll hit chu up later."

Miranda didn't say anything in response. She didn't even look at Black Vic to acknowledge that he had even said anything. She waved her empty hand over her shoulder at him. It was the only concession that she made to seeing Black Vic off and out of her presence.

BLACK Vic closed the door to the apartment behind him and left Miranda to slip out of his mind as he took the stairs, two at a time, to the bottom floor. Once he was in the parking lot, he didn't even glance back up to see if Miranda was still on her balcony, watching him leave, as he went to join Echo and Bingo at the car. It was alright that he didn't look back. There would have been no one for him to see anyway. Miranda had long since moved back into her apartment and secured the sliding balcony door behind her as she went in.

Black Vic clasped hands with Echo as he neared the car. They came together for a brief moment; long enough to pat each other on the back as part of their ritual greeting.

"We good, brah?" Black Vic asked as he released Echo's hand.

Bingo was still sitting in the backseat of the car so Black Vic didn't give him the same customary greeting that he had given to Echo. Echo responded with a smile. He answered as he was opening the driver's door to get into the car.

"Yeah, man. Butta, straight butta," said Echo.

Bingo chimed in from the inside of the car and said, "don't forget da 'bread', man. Ya heard?", meaning the money that they had stolen, and then he laughed at his own joke.

Echo climbed into the car and pointed to the backseat of the car after Black Vic had gotten in and closed the door.

Black Vic looked over the top of the front seat into the rear section of the car. Bingo was sitting in the backseat behind Black Vic and on his left hand side, there sat about seven bricks of Marijuana, wrapped in clear plastic with clear packing tape binding the entirety of each block closed. A duffle bag was sitting in his lap. Bingo opened it up and showed Black Vic the contents when Black Vic had finally looked in his direction. The inside of the duffle bag contained bundles of US currency, wrapped up with rubber bands.

Each bundle contained more bills, each of the same denomination, so that there where rolls of tens, twenties, fifties, and hundreds. It was not as much money as it seemed because there were more bundles of the tens than there were of any other denomination. The bag contained enough bundles of money so that the bag appeared to contain approximately thirty to forty thousand dollars in dirty, ill gotten, drug money. Black Vic was pleased and the oily smile that snaked across his face indicated that.

"Did ya have to ventilate da place?" asked Black Vic as he turned back around in his seat.

Echo answered him, saying, "naw. When Bingo pulled da pole, Duke's man went and pissed hisself. He cried like a bitch too."

Bingo laughed and Echo joined in on the joke. It was just another game to them. The everyday violence and danger on the street was just a part of the life that they had learned to deal with at an early age. It meant nothing to them to have your life hanging in the balance between this world and the next. It was pretty simple. When you *had* nothing, you *cared for* nothing.

The only determining factor of losing your life in these streets was whether the person holding the gun felt like pulling that trigger or not. That was the life that they had come to expect out on the hard streets of Atlanta.

Echo put the car in gear and drove off. Bingo tapped Black Vic on the shoulder and passed him a lit blunt. Black Vic took a few drags and passed it on to Echo when he was done.

"Bingo," called out Black Vic. "Do ya know where Duke is tonight?" Black Vic had the urge to rub salt on a wound that he knew Duke was unaware of so far as he knew.

"Gimme a minute, ya heard?" said Bingo.

He pulled out his cell phone and made a call to someone that he knew. A few minutes later, he hung up the phone and put it back into the pants pocket that he had pulled it out of.

"My bro Issac said he saw Duke's car over at da Laugh Factory, ya heard?" Bingo eventually reported.

Black Vic nodded and then he tapped Echo on his shoulder and pointed out of the car window. Echo understood the message clearly enough and took the next street that would put them in the right direction to get where Black Vic wanted them to go.

With the way that Echo was driving, it only took them about half of an hour to get from where they were, on the side of town where Miranda lived, to the comedy club. Echo found a parking spot a little ways away from the front of the club and the three of them left the car to go inside of the club so that Black Vic could find Duke. Once the three of them were in the club, it didn't take long for them to find where Duke was. He was sitting in a booth next to Sunny, when they located him.

Black Vic stopped in front of the booth. From where he and his friends were standing, they blocked the flow of the people around them that were trying to get by so that they had to stand and wait to get through until Black Vic and his boys moved out of the way.

"Lookie what we got here," said Black Vic to Echo and Bingo.

Black Vic played up his surprised astonishment at seeing Duke for those few people who happened to be around them and within hearing distance. His primary goal was to provoke Duke, a deliberate effort to incite a reaction. Simultaneously, he aimed to showcase his assertiveness to the members under his influence. He believed that maintaining control over them necessitated a demonstration of dominance over those he perceived as less powerful. This mindset adhered to the principle of survival of the fittest, with the conviction that the strongest should naturally assume leadership, a philosophy deeply embedded in his psyche.

"If it ain't da fairy and his boyfriend," said Black Vic. "Now I wonder which one's da fairy and which one's da boyfriend," Black Vic continued while first pointing at Duke and then Sunny as he spoke. "I guess it don't matter none. Both of 'em is punks."

Duke immediately took offense at everything that Black Vic had said.

"What da fuck did chu just say to me, nigga?" asked Duke, coming partway off of the seat that he was in.

Sunny restrained Duke with moderate difficulty. It took both hands, and a little force, to hold him back.

Black Vic looked directly at Sunny and asked, "that's yo boyfriend, right?"

Sunny ignored the question and struggled with Duke to get him to sit back down again after Black Vic had worked him up.

"What chu want, nigga?" asked Duke.

"Me?" said Black Vic, pointing at himself and feigning innocence. "I just came to see da show," he said while pointing over his shoulder at the stage behind him.

Black Vic was pointing up at the stage to the comedian who was currently up there and struggling to keep the attention of the audience on his performance — despite Black Vic's raised, distracting voice — instead of the commotion that Black Vic and Duke were causing. Black Vic leaned in towards Duke over the table that separated the both of them. He spoke quietly and conspiratorially with Duke. "By da way, did yo man's get da chance to change out of dem pissy clothes?"

Duke swung his fist at Black Vic's face but Black Vic was too fast for him and pulled back before he could connect with the punch he had thrown. He shrugged off the restraining hand that Sunny had on him and came from around the table towards Black Vic.

Duke had gotten the call about the robbery but was going to wait to respond to it because he was with Sunny. Duke's face twisted in anger.

"Did chu rob me, nigga?" asked Duke as he came from the booth.

Duke had broken free from Sunny's restraining grasp. He didn't wait for a response from Black Vic, but instead balled up his fists and got ready to swing again. Before he could react, he caught a punch from his blind side. He fell backwards into the booth, on top of Sunny. He looked up and saw Echo smiling down at him.

Duke shook Sunny off of him again and was about to lift up his shirt when the bouncers showed up and stopped the confrontation from advancing any further than it already had. The bouncers took charge of the tense situation and ended up escorting Duke, Black Vic, Bingo, and Echo up out of the club. Sunny followed close behind Duke in his attempt to try and keep Duke from getting into any further difficulties due to an increase of the hostilities between him and Black Vic.

Sunny wanted Duke to remain safe and unharmed and that was all that he really cared for. He was concerned by the move Duke had begun to make inside the club. The move that ended up being aborted just at the arrival of the bouncers at their table. It looked to him as if Duke had been about to brandish a firearm of some kind. He didn't want something like that to occur and wind up getting Duke killed in the process; or anyone else for that matter.

For Sunny, the anger that abounded due to the current issues caused by the altercation at the table could in no way justify the loss of anyone's life by any means. Sunny wanted to do what he could do to try and keep Duke safe and alive. That meant anything short of giving up his own life for a dumb reason.

A crowd ended up gathering around the confrontation between Black Vic and Duke so that by the time that the bounces had arrived to the area, there were a decent amount of spectators abounding. The group followed the procession out of the club in order to continue to observe the drama unfolding between the two combatants. Sunny tried to follow closely to stay near to Duke but he found that hard for him to do. He had started out at a disadvantage what with him having to work his way out from behind the table in the booth.

Sunny tried to rush his way out through the crowd, pushing where he could and ducking around other individuals if he was able or needed to. He was not making any type of great progress or headway in getting to the front of the crowd and near to Duke. He could just make out Duke's form from over the heads of those few individuals that were now gathered between him and his objective and target of reaching Duke.

Sunny was not able to get to the front of that throng of bodies until he was well beyond the front doors of the comedy club and outside standing in the asphalt parking lot. The scene opened up horribly before him as he took in the images in front of him.

The bouncer's arm was stretched out, trying — without having to exert much effort to do so — to keep the crowd back from the madness that was beginning to unfold. Most of the spectators were content with staying at the fringes of the drama. Many others took the chance to find a way to distance themselves from the chaos that was unfolding in front of the club. These individuals either chose to go back into the relative safety of the interior of the comedy club or they instead decided that it was a better idea to leave and vacate the area all together so that they could be far away if the situation deteriorated any further than it already had.

Sunny stood there in the parking lot, just before the entrance to the club, and watched in horror as Duke used the semi automatic pistol in his hand to beat Black Vic in the face. Bingo and Echo stood by watching. When it looked as if one of them would move, Duke would point the gun at them.

The sun had dipped below the horizon by the time they left exited the club, leaving the city wrapped in shadows. As Duke and Black Vic faced off, the streetlights cast long silhouettes, a stark contrast to the sunny facade they presented earlier. The fading sunlight mirrored the descent into their darker, dangerous world.

"Stay da fuck right dere," said Duke to Echo and Bingo, then he looked back down at the bloody mess that was Black Vic. "What was dat shit chu was sayin' in da club, nigga?" Duke demanded of Black Vic.

When Black Vic didn't respond, Duke smacked him in the face again with the pistol.

"You wanna steal from me, huh, bitch?" screamed Duke, then he pointed the gun at Black Vic's head. "I oughta smoke yo bitch ass, right here, right now."

Black Vic's hands shot up to fend off Duke's blows and to signify his intent to surrender.

"Nah, nah. It's cool, man," Black Vic said through bloody lips as Duke continued to press the semi automatic pistol into his cheek. "Yo shit's in da car."

Black Vic turned to look at Echo. "Give 'em da damn keys," Black Vic slurred through his split lip at Echo.

Echo reached into his pocket to fetch out the keys to the car. He chirped the alarm and threw the keys to Duke. The keys landed on the asphalt by Duke's feet.

Black Vic reached over and scraped up the keys off of the ground, digging his nails into the asphalt in his rush to get them. He presented them to Duke. "Here, man. All yo shit's in da car. It's all dere, brah."

Duke snatched the keys from Black Vic with his free hand, all without removing the pistol from Black Vic's cheek. He looked around until he made eye contact with Sunny. He tossed the keys at Sunny, who caught them on reflex.

"Go get da car," he said to Sunny.

Sunny found himself numbly obeying Duke, even though it was the last thing in the world that he wanted to do. He didn't want anything to do with this violence. He didn't want to be involved. This was not who he was. This was not what he wanted in his life but he did what Duke asked him to do anyway.

It didn't take long for Sunny to get the car to the front door of the club after he eventually located it. When he got out of the driver's seat, Duke tossed him the keys to his own car. He came over to Sunny while keeping his gun pointed towards Black Vic and his two friends, Echo and Bingo. Sunny moved out of his way.

"Get in," Duke said to Sunny.

Sunny shook his head no. "I don't think so, Duke. I don't want anything to do with what's going on here."

Duke cocked his head to the side and narrowed his eyes. "What chu say? You ain't gettin' in?"

"No, Duke. I don't wanna get involved with this," Sunny said while waving his arm to take in the situation.

"Chu don't wanna get involved? Nigga, dis shit yo damn *fault*. Chu da one said chu wanted to be wit' me. Dis is what I fucking *do*! Dis is who I fucking *am*! If chu don't wanna be wit' me den chu can get da fuck on."

Duke snatched his keys back from Sunny. He got in Black Vic's car. He looked over at Sunny and waited. Sunny crossed his arms over his chest and glanced away from Duke, at the asphalt beneath his feet. Duke made a disgusted noise with his mouth and put the car in gear. He looked over at Black Vic.

"Dis shit ain't over, bitch ass nigga," he called out.

Duke turned to Sunny once more and waited. When it was pretty clear that Sunny was not going to change his mind, he let off the brake and began to roll out of the parking lot, leaving Sunny behind him and the mess that he had helped to make. Siren's from police cars sounded off in the night, getting louder as they drew nearer. Duke disappeared into the city night. Echo and Bingo helped Black Vic to leave the area before the police got there and started asking questions that they were reluctant to answer.

7

Sunny went back into the club when he was done answering questions that the police presented to him. They were interested in the particulars of what had occurred and who the relevant players were in that drama. It didn't take much explaining of who the actors were before Sunny was certain that the police officers knew who Sunny and the other witnesses were talking about. The description of the suspects deportment and of their physical characteristics was enough. That was easily added to the names that were presented to the police in order for them to make a more substantial identification.

The club manager, Mike, cut Sunny off as he entered the lobby of the club. Mike cornered him. "I don't need this at my club, Sunny. You got a promising future ahead of you but you're gonna have to get your personal shit together and keep it out of my club, if you wanna keep working and performing here."

Mike walked off when he was done, leaving a stunned and numb Sunny in his wake . He hadn't given Sunny a chance to respond to what he had said at all. Sunny leaned on the wall that was behind him and exhaled slowly. He didn't realize that he had been holding in his breath. His shoulders drooped low as his breath escaped his body.

His chest ached. His tense hands unclenched from the balled up fists that he had been carrying around since the end of the incident between Duke and Black Vic. When Sunny took his next breath, his whole body shuddered. He pushed himself off of the wall that he had been leaning on during the talk with Mike and he wiped hastily at his eyes with the back of his hands. Sunny got to the bar and ordered a strong drink; he wanted it strong so that it could have an impact and to strap some steel on his backbone before his emotions got the better of him.

Duke's actions rocked Sunny to the core of his being. He was having some serious issues trying to reconcile the differences between how dangerous Duke was with how he was when it was just him and Sunny together. It didn't seem possible to him that the man that he loved could be so cold. How the man that he loved could be so cruel. How the man that he loved could be so brutal.

That just was not the man that he was used to. But the truth of it was right there in his face, if he would just choose to not be blind to it. Open his eyes so that he could see that ugly truth. Maybe then he would be able to fortify his heart so that he could move on. That is what Sunny felt like he really needed to do to resolve this whole mess; get away from the drama and extricate himself from the madness so that sanity could reign, once more, in his life.

Sunny killed the shot in front of him and ordered another round. Not for the first time in his entire life, Sunny wondered why it was that he was also feeling like he was traveling in circles. He would get comfortable with being who he was. Comfortable being in his own skin. This allowed him to meet someone new in his life. This always seemed to be followed by a period where he would have a lot of drama show up in his life and he would end up back in a place where he questioned who he was and what he wanted. The beginning of the cycle started up again after that point. He felt like he was circling the drain and about to be washed out with the rest of the dirty water.

The new shot of liquor in front of Sunny was consumed again, rather swiftly. He ordered, and received, yet another replacement. Sunny started to get antsy. He got angry as his thoughts began to betray him. Even though that betrayal was only to himself. He was concerned with why he should care so much for a person who obviously didn't value who he was.

His investment was definitely not giving him the return that he had expected and it was not fair. He cared so much and could not seem to even get a portion of that back in return. Not in a way that he believed that he deserved. So he asked himself where was this going? What was this leading to? Sunny was pretty sure that he had an answer for those two particular questions.

He didn't like the answers that were being presented. He was destined to soon be single again. Sunny took his shot. He waved his hand at the bartender and received a fresh shot, nice and neat. He downed it and another took the place of the empty one.

In just a few short days, Duke had hurt Sunny twice. The first was because Duke denied who he was in front of Sunny and Black Vic, which left Sunny trying to figure out what his place was in Duke's life. He didn't want to be just some 'dirty little secret' that Duke could hide away if things got too embarrassing for him. Sunny felt like he deserved a hell of a lot more than that from a relationship and he was right.

Sunny knew that he deserved more than that out of a relationship. He was determined not to settle for less than total and complete inclusion and openness in a relationship. Sunny could see no real valid reason why he should not be able to get what he believed that he deserved from a relationship. If he was willing to give his partner his all and more. If he could do that then he was going to want that — no, he was going to demand to get that same thing in total and complete reciprocation. No if's, and's, or but's.

Sunny had an elbow resting on the bar and he placed his head into the hand of that arm. He took a deep breath and let it out slowly. He used his hand to scratch his head. His reflections about his own immediate concerns had blinded him to his environment so that he was not really aware when someone sat down next to him at the bar. Sunny reached out absently for his next shot and came up short when his searching fingers collided with someone else's. Sunny looked up in surprise. He hadn't expected to find a hand waiting for him. He was greeted by a generous smile from a beautiful hispanic male with a dimple in his right cheek.

"Hey. I'm Robert Hernandez but you can call me Bobby," said Bobby.

Sunny was stunned. He could not figure out what to say in response to Bobby's greeting. There were too many other thoughts rushing around in his head. Sunny was also stunned by the response of his body to this handsome man sitting beside him at the bar. The last thing that Sunny had expected this night, after all that had happened, wes to have to worry about his heart rate speeding up unexpectedly.

"Hi," stumbled out Sunny.

"I know you've had a rough night. I saw all of that. Drinking won't make it any better though."

Sunny gave a rueful smile and withdrew his hand from Bobby's hand. "You saw that train wreck?"

"Yeah," Bobby smiled gently in response.

Sunny groaned and dropped his head back into his hand so that he could hide his face in shame. This was not the way that Sunny had hoped to become infamous in the world. He didn't want to be known as the upcoming, new star with the crazy relationship. He was not sure if there was even anyone in the world who would choose to have something like that attached to them being known. That was not a way that Sunny wanted to make a name for hisself.

Sunny was still trying to deal with the fallout from the scene between Duke and Black Vic. Now he was sitting here with the handsome guy that had helped to give him validation as a performer a few weeks prior. He didn't know what to do so he decided to just play it cool and just see where things went from there.

Sunny now had to worry about his crumbling relationship and the impact that it might have on his developing career. He appreciated the distraction that Bobby offered with his presence. It was nice to just forget the madness of the world and just talk for no real purpose but to enjoy someone else's presence.

Sunny knew what he was going to have to do in regards to his relationship with Duke. He was going to have to let it go. He was going to have to stop letting himself be led on. He was going to have to stop for his on good. He was going to have to stop sugar coating the disfunctionality of the poisonous relationship that he had with Duke and get away with what little sanity he had left. He was going to have to run and not walk, away from his ties to Duke.

There was nothing to be gained by staying where he was as a person. It served no real purpose. There was no great growth involved if he did choose to stay where he was with Duke. He was going to establish a new normal for himself because he needed to take care of himself and attend to his growth.

But again, Sunny felt as if he was running around in circles. He wanted to scream. He was more frustrated because he felt like someone or something had smothered the flames of his new relationship with heaps of wet dirt. It felt like that dirt was clinging all over him. There was not one part of him that felt clean. He felt filthy from the top of his head to the bottom of his feet.

Gathering his courage together, Sunny knew what course of action he was going to finally have to come to terms with. It was a decision that he should have realized long ago. The decision had always been there, just barely hidden in the background shadows of his drama filled night.

Now it was staring at him head on and he could no longer avoid his headlong collision with the future. He was going to have to give up on Duke because no other choice made sense if he was to remain sane and emotionally stable. He was not willing to risk his well being in that regard for no one. No one, unless he loved them just as deeply as he loved his father, Peter and his best friend Miranda.

Sunny resigned himself to his decision and then he decided to just try and enjoy the company of the man that was sitting right next to him. At least this man had a beautiful smile. Sunny stayed where he was and pushed his troubles to the back of his mind. He kept Bobby company and they both enjoyed the rest of the evening's performers. He left and went home by himself a few hours later. He felt content about his acceptance of the decision he had reached. Spending time just sitting and chatting with Bobby had also served to calm him down and help him center himself.

Sunny knew that he had tripped. He had fallen down but he was more than capable of making the decision to get up and to keep pushing forward. He was now determined to make sure that he saw his dreams and goals realized. Why should he feel any the least bit like this set back was a failure? It was a learning lesson.

Even if it was a failure it was not like it was the only failure he had in his life. This was not a life-changing failure. This was a defining failure and what he meant by that thought was that the failure would help him sharpen his focus. He could hone the blade of his life to help him cut through other challenges that he was bound to face in time. Events that would challenge him further in the future. In time. Down the road.

As Sunny faced his relationship struggles, he felt like he was trapped in the darkness just before dawn, waiting for the sun to bring clarity. Bobby served to help Sunny stop worrying about things that he could not change. With little chance of affecting a change in his circumstances, there was little to no need to continue caring. He didn't have to deposit the remainder of his life into Duke's hands. He could move on. He was young and just really starting out with his life. He was only just now beginning to see what man he was going to develop into.

He might not be ready to fall back in love so soon but he was sure that he was ready to make a new friend. Bobby made it easy to determine whether or not Sunny was going to open up, one way or another. Just like that, they both kept each other focused on how life was unfolding right in front of them, instead of what got them there at that point, they focused on 'right then'. They spent the rest of the night companionably. Both of them laughed when it was appropriate to. They didn't go too heavily on the alcohol. Sunny's reason dealt with a need to get himself back home to his own particular residence later on that evening when they left at the end of the night.

8

Despite the rocky start that Sunny had endured on that Friday night, he had ended up being able to set aside his worries for the rest of that night. Meeting up with Bobby had been a godsend to his level of overall sanity. That Friday night had started off as a nightmare and he just wanted to forget about it and all of the trouble that had been brought along with it.

As Sunny faced his relationship struggles, he felt like he was trapped in the darkness just before dawn, waiting for the sun to bring clarity. He had gotten to the club this second night of the weekend hoping that things would somehow work out better than they had the previous night. He would be grateful if that would happen and nothing untoward occurred to ruin this night for him as well.

Tonight he was expected to be the head act, so he had prepared a lot more material for this set than he normally gave during the other performances. Those sets that he had given since he had started performing at the club. Sunny looked around at the crowd that was already present at the club. He was not looking for anyone in particular and didn't really know why this specific night he was so interested in the makeup of the audience.

Sunny stopped at the bar and decided to have a glass of wine instead of his customary shot of tequila. He sat down at the bar and just took the time to people watch. He still was not really sure that he was looking for something certain or not. Regardless of what he was searching for, he found solace and relaxation in the act of just being one more face in the midst of the crowd for the time being. Before the spotlight projected out and made him the center of attention.

Sunny stayed posted where he was at the bar. He got through by nursing an additional glass of wine as he watched the acts of his contemporaries and cohorts in the business. He was due to be on stage and perform at the end of the act that he was currently watching. It was not until Sunny saw Bobby smiling at him and walking up to the bar to sit down beside him that he realized who it was that he had been looking for all night long. Sunny felt himself crushing on Bobby's dimple as the young man drew nearer to him.

"I didn't get here too late, did I?" Bobby asked as he neared closer enough to Sunny to be heard without really having to be too loud and distract the other patrons nearby that were enjoying the show.

"Too late for what?" Sunny asked.

He scrunched up his nose and his eyebrows dipped low with his smile. "To see *you* on stage."

"Oh," Sunny exclaimed. As often as he had seen Bobby at the club recently, he hadn't thought that Bobby was coming specifically to see him performing up there on that stage and before that spotlight. It made Sunny feel a little more than warm inside and he could not hide how it had affected him to hear that due to the enormous grin on his face. The warmth of the slight wine buzz he had going on didn't help.

Sunny immediately blamed the drink for that. He put the half finished glass on the flat surface of the bar and determined that he would avoid anymore libations for the remainder of the evening. He was refusing to be embarrassed again by a revealing, uncontrollable reaction to something that Bobby might decide to say later on in the evening.

Sunny was rather pleased with himself. He was now aware that he had his own dedicated fan. His personal cheering section, in addition to Miranda. His thought about her, and how they had last parted, served to threaten to derail his good humor for the evening, so he instead let thoughts of his best friend in the world slip away from his mind for the time being. He could worry about mending that fence at a later date. Right now, he wanted to focus only on the handsome man that sat beside him and smiled at him with that cute, lopsided smile topped with that single dimple.

Sunny had to stop and take a mental step back from the current situation. The current meeting with such a nice guy. He had to pause because he really was not certain if his new friend understood or knew that he was gay. He didn't hide who he was or the fact that he was gay in his act. Even still, he just wanted to make certain that Bobby had an understanding of his sexual orientation. He didn't want it to be something that could potentially come between the two of them, as it seemed to be doing with his most recent relationship. There really was no reason that he knew of why things should have turned out the way that they had other than Duke was not comfortable with letting the world know that he was gay.

He decided to just throw it out there so that it was known. "You know I'm gay, don't you?" asked Sunny.

He smiled hopefully at Bobby and was dismayed when he saw the smile disappear from Bobby's face.

"I mean it's not like I've tried to hide it or anything like that. I use that in my act because its true."

Bobby was still regarding Sunny with a skeptical look so Sunny didn't know how to respond to the awkward silence that now hung between them, heavy like a wet curtain. Sunny cleared his throat and shuffled around on the bar stool, trying to adjust his seat. The seconds crept by and Sunny hoped that something — anything, would break the tension in that naked silence.

A grin blossomed on Bobby's face. Sunny released a sigh. It seemed like everything was destined to be alright with them. Bobby patted Sunny on his shoulder.

"Everything's gonna be alright," said Bobby easily. "I knew that already and it's not an issue."

Sunny playfully punched Bobby in the chest and said, "you had me worried there for a few minutes. I thought that you didn't know that and it was gonna be a problem because I just said something about it."

"You didn't have to worry. I'm gay too."

Sunny's eyes bulged. He was not totally thrown but he was pleased to hear the revelation. "I thought that you bought that shot of tequila long ago for my friend Miranda. That first night we saw you."

"I did," Bobby said quickly. He waited for a response from Sunny and decided that he should let Sunny off of the hook when he saw the confused look on his face.

"I was joking. You looked so serious when you said that, so I couldn't help myself. I had to say it," Bobby said as he laughed at Sunny's discomfiture.

"You're not funny," Sunny grumbled.

"That's why *I'm* not the comedian here. But you *are* funny." He leaned over and kissed Sunny. Sunny was surprised by the softness of the kiss. Bobby's lips fluttered on his own like a butterfly landing on a flower petal.

When Bobby eventually backed off from Sunny, Sunny brought two fingers up to his lips and left them there. He wanted to feel those soft lips again but he could not figure out how to ask for more without him seeming to be too greedy and needy. The last thing in the world that he wanted was to do something that might end up, in some way, scaring off Bobby when things had just gotten so deliciously interesting.

It was like sunbeams parted the clouds after a rain storm and Sunny wanted to stay bathed in that sunlight for as long as he possibly could. For as long as was humanly possible. As long as Bobby would allow him to remain there. That sunlight was warming to his heart and it filled his soul with some small amount of hope and joy.

"You've got a set to do, don't you?" Bobby asked.

Sunny shook the cobwebs out of his head. Bobby was distracting him. Even though his troubles were the thing he was being distracted from, it was still a distraction that he didn't need right before he gave his performance.

"Yes," said Sunny.

Sunny glanced at his watch to mark the time. He still had just a few more minutes before he was due on stage to do his own skit. He reached over and picked up his glass and finished off the last little bit of it.

Bobby put his hand on Sunny's shoulder. He said, "good luck. I'm sure you'll do great up there."

"Aren't you staying for the show? I don't want you to miss my act."

Bobby shook his head sadly. "No, unfortunately I won't be able to stay and watch you."

"Why'd you come then?"

"I was hoping that I'd see you for a moment before you went on tonight. I wanted to give you something."

"You already gave me something nice," said Sunny as he touched his fingers to his lips again.

Bobby's eyes drifted away with his gentle smile cresting on his full and succulent, honey colored lips. "I wanted to give you that and something else."

"Well I gotta say that I definitely appreciate the first of what you meant to give me." Sunny hesitated. He was not brave enough, just yet, to keep speaking so candidly so he took a deep breath and let it out softly. He waited until he felt calm enough to continue. "So what's the other thing that you wanted me to have?"

Bobby didn't say anything but instead he just moved into quick and determined action that would end up revealing whatever else that it was that he actually wanted to gift to Sunny. Bobby called the bartender over to where the both of them were. Sunny thought that maybe Bobby was going to order them a drink or something. He was pleased when, instead of ordering a drink for both of them, Bobby asked instead for the bartender to lend him a pen that he might take a moment to put to the use that he had in mind. He grabbed up a cocktail napkin and proceeded to use it, and the pen, to inscribe his contact information into a more permanent medium. He presented this to Sunny.

Bobby got up from the barstool and passed the pen that he had borrowed back to the bartender from whom he had acquired it. He stepped close to Sunny. In between Sunny's legs. He placed his hands gently on each side of his face and pulled him in close. Bobby matched his lips up tight against Sunny's lips. It was not rushed. There was no urgency in the act. Bobby parted Sunny's lips with his tongue and probed and played with Sunny's own tongue before he pulled away, leaving a bewildered Sunny behind.

"Good luck tonight. I gotta go. Give me a call tomorrow," said Bobby.

Bobby brushed Sunny's lips with his finger tips and then touched his cheek. Bobby gave a broad smile and left Sunny behind with his muddled thoughts to contend with.

Sunny watched Bobby as he walked out of the club. He absently ran his fingers across his lips that had been gently used and left bruised with the blush of his blood rushing to them. He turned to the bartender when she said, 'Damn, that was hot.'

Sunny dipped his head and his light colored cheeks got a lot rosier than they had been just a while ago. He was not going to forget that moment anytime soon, that was for certain. Sunny actually let himself consider the thought of whether or not he and Bobby could last together if things between them even had the chance to get that far.

Sunny found himself fighting off pretty raunchy thoughts. He was wondering how good Bobby would look wearing one of his shirts. He was now so thoroughly distracted that he completely missed his cue and initial call to the stage. The club MC had to call out to him again and even then, it took the spotlight operator reorienting the light beam so that he was bathed in the revealing illumination, and awash with its glare, before he was able to get his head to descend from the clouds and bring him back to the earth and the reality that was around him.

Sunny started, waved at the audience, and got up from the bar. He made his way up to the stage and apologized to his audience before he got started in on his set of material. He hit the heights that he was aiming for and skyrocketed to the stratosphere. The crowd loved him. They adored him. Sunny had to take care to pay attention to what it was that he was doing. He didn't want to mess up the timing of his material just because he really could not get his mind off of what had just recently happened. Happy thoughts of Bobby kept trying to get in the way of remembering the material of his act.

It all worked out fine in the end though. He was eventually able to get through his performance without too many serious incidents happening to cause his act to bomb. The audience seemed to pick up on the fact that he was distracted and so he just decided to try his best and incorporate that nervous energy into the execution of his act. The audience responded well to this strategy.

Sunny departed from the stage to a roar of applause from the gathered crowd. They were exuberant in their praise of Sunny's performance. It was obvious that he had talent and had a knack for knowing how to move the crowd. He had returned once to the stage after an uproars standing ovation. He would have gone back up onstage for a third time but he had no more material and he didn't feel like pressing his luck with his attentive audience.

Sunny shook hands and accepted pats on the back with their accompanying congratulations as he made his way off the stage and through the throng of spectators. His peers congratulated his efforts as well. He was slowly making his way to the bar where he had planned on grabbing a place to sit himself before the weariness of his performance overtook him. He was also anxious to get a shot of tequila to celebrate his reception by the audience. He sat down at the bar after what seemed to him like ages trying to get through the crowd. The club manager, Mike, sidled up next to him.

"You did a great job, kid. Keep it up," said Mike before he moved off to disappear amid the crowded floor of the club. The night for the club was drawing to a close and he had work to do.

Sunny ordered his shot and downed it. He reached into the pocket of his pants and retrieved the cocktail napkin that he had stuffed into it earlier. He unfolded it and stared at the neat, printed script that was written on it. A name and a telephone number. That was all that was there, but it was enough. Those two written lines, the names and the digits written there; those two marched off into two singularly neat lines and were exactly enough to put a smile onto Sunny's face yet again and to cause Sunny to raise his fingers up to his lips to cover that smile and to perhaps recapture that moment when his lips had been held captive, just briefly.

All-in-all, what was held on the cocktail napkin was enough to kindle hope and desire. A hope that maybe the future held something nice and also pleasant for him. A hope that maybe this was where he was supposed to have been in the first place. That cocktail napkin's promise made desire all too real for Sunny. It made the presence of his powerful desire a force in his life that could no longer be pushed to the wayside and ignored.

These two feelings of hope and desire carried Sunny through the rest of the evening. The feelings helped him to keep the smile on his face as he left the club on that late night evening to make his way back home along the city streets. The feelings were more of a bonus in this regard because he was still soaring in the heavens because of the reception of his audience. That was more of a high for him than any drug that he might have taken. The two feelings that had been evoked by the contents of that cocktail napkin and the promises that it held eventually carried Sunny home safely where he went about his nightly routine and turned in for the night.

SUNNY woke up that Sunday morning to sunlight streaming through his curtained window and splashing down on his face in a pleasant warmth like the sun was embracing him after a long night's slumber. Before he began to move, his thoughts trickled back to that moment before he got up on the stage to perform the night previous. He again tapped his finger tips gently to his lips and blushed hotly. A smile broke across his face and spread out to be seen from each side of his presently poised fingers.

He wondered if it was too early to use the numbers that he had been given. Sunny wanted to reach out and get a hold of Bobby so that he could drown in that man's deep brown eyes. Thoughts of feeling those tender lips pressed against his own somehow found a way into the forefront of his thoughts as well.

Sunny's happy disposition began to sour a little bit and his smile began to droop in response. This thing with Bobby was the kind of thing you went to share with your best friend. Your best friend would be happy with you and would be able to easily help you figure out if it was too early in the day to use a number you had gotten the night previously. The only problem for Sunny right then was the fact that he and his best friend were not currently on speaking terms.

Sunny looked at the time on his cell phone. It was only ten minutes past nine. He had slept later than he normally did. He decided to throw caution to the winds and give in partially to his desire to use the number that he had been given. Instead of calling, he sent a text message instead. He put the phone down after he sent the message and then he started to get out of bed so that he could get ready for the day.

He had barely gotten his feet onto the floor when he got a notification that he had received a text message. It didn't take Sunny long to realize that it was a reply from Bobby. He wondered what

Bobby was doing this early in the morning. He had obviously responded rather quickly to just be getting up for the day like Sunny was.

Sunny had no sooner picked up his phone and read the good morning reply that he had received in response to his morning greeting when his phone started ringing. It was Bobby calling and Sunny eagerly connected by answering the call.

"Good morning," said Sunny.

"Hey," came Bobby's easy response. "Are you busy today?" he asked quickly.

Sunny was surprised but answered as soon as he recovered from the abrupt question and how it took him unaware.

"No, I don't really have anything I was gonna do today. What? Did you have something in mind?" Sunny asked hopefully.

"Just text me your address and get ready to go somewhere. I'll send you a text to let you know how long it will take for me to get there once I get your address."

Bobby didn't wait for a response before he went ahead and hung up the call with Sunny. It was pretty obvious to Sunny that Bobby was sure that they could hang out together that day.

Sunny sent his address to Bobby in a text message and received a reply that Bobby would be at his house to pick him up in about forty five minutes. He admonished Sunny to be ready to go when he got there. That was enough to get Sunny up and about the task of getting prepared for the day.

He was looking forward to seeing Bobby. He was looking forward to it so much so that even his dad noticed the good mood that he was in and had even commented on his son's perky behavior. Sunny gave his dad a hug and slipped the coffee mug his dad had out of his dad's hand.

He was already in his room with the door closed when his dad mourned the loss of his coffee mug and lamenting its loss, he complained. His father didn't complain — too loudly, about his cup being purloined. Instead, he shook his head and returned to the kitchen to get another cup of joe.

It was to no use complaining because Sunny already had music playing in his room so Peter went to the kitchen to make another cup of coffee for himself and hope that this time he could actually keep it in his hands and get a chance to drink the wonderful, god given creation.

It didn't take much longer before Sunny was ready to go. It was just before eleven and already the city was heating up. It was promising to be a hot day so Sunny was ready with a pair of bluejeans shorts and a graphic t-shirt. He was not really sure if what he was wearing would be appropriate for what Bobby might have planned for them to do for the day but he was not worried. If he had to change into something else then it would not take him long to do so.

Sunny was outside in the front of his house when Bobby pulled up in front, driving a large, four door pickup truck. When Sunny saw his smile, and that single dimple, he felt like he could get in that truck and run away with Bobby to wherever it was that he wanted to go that day. He opened the door of the passenger side of the truck and climbed in.

Bobby leaned across the interior of the truck and planted a quick kiss on the cheek of Sunny. Sunny was not ready for it. He was still fumbling around with his seatbelt when it happened. He didn't mind, in fact he wished that he had received the kiss on his lips instead of on his cheek. Sunny felt like he was robbed but he was still floating away on the wings of doves. He could not help but to smile broadly. Bobby put the truck into gear and drove off.

"Where are we going?" asked Sunny.

Country music played softly through the speakers of the truck. Sunny was not expecting Bobby to be a fan of country music but then he admonished himself for his preconceived notion of the type of person who would listen to a specific type of music.

"I'm gonna show you where I work."

"Oh," Sunny said in surprise. "Okay."

"After that, I was thinking we could do lunch in midtown."

"That sounds good. So where do you work?"

Bobby laughed pleasantly. He reached behind him, into the backseat, and brought forward a camouflaged jacket. It had Bobby's last name on it and lieutenant bars sewn on. Sunny turned the jacket over in his hands until the other nametape was in view. It had US Airforce sewn on it.

"You're in the military?"

"Yeah. I'm stationed at the airbase that's north of Atlanta. That's where we're going first, then we'll come back down southward to get to midtown Atlanta."

"Sounds good to me," said Sunny.

He sat back and enjoyed the ride up north, along the slightly busy freeway, towards the north of the city of Atlanta. As they rode through the downtown area, Sunny watched the buildings slip by and fall off behind them as they continued on. Most of those buildings belonged to the state college that had just recently become a university. It was a nice ride and it was relaxing to Sunny.

"Do you like country music?" Bobby asked after a few minutes of silence that followed between them.

Sunny turned from looking outside of the passenger window, and instead, adjusted the focus of his attention to Bobby. "Yeah. I like some stuff."

"I can change the station if you'd like."

"No, that's alright," said Sunny. He paused a moment and decided that it was time to try and learn a little bit more about lieutenant Bobby Distra. "So how long have you been in the Airforce?"

Bobby looked over at him and smiled. He turned back towards the front so that he could pay attention to the traffic out on the road with them and around them. "I went in after I graduated college. I've been in for about a year and a half now. Closer to two now."

"Are you planning on making a career out of the military?" Sunny asked. "It's twenty years for a retirement, right?"

"Yeah, something like that. Twenty years makes a full career and then you can retire. I'm not sure yet if I want to do that or not. I guess it just depends. That's a big decision to make."

"What could it possibly depend on? I mean you retire and get a check for the rest of your life from what I understand. If its twenty years and you join at twenty, then you can get a retirement check starting in your forties."

"You make it sound great when you say it like that but its not that easy."

"What's not that easy about it?"

"Well, like I said, it depends. The military is a huge commitment and it demands your time, with few exceptions, if any. No matter what."

"So, you still haven't made it sound like a challenging choice to me yet about deciding to do twenty years."

Bobby cocked his head to the side as he thought of how to form his response to Sunny. "The military life is hard on families. If both partners aren't on the same sheet of music, with an understanding of what it takes to be in the military, or be a military spouse, then they might not make it as a couple through the whole twenty years."

"Oh, I didn't know it was like that. I guess it would suck to be with someone whose always leaving and stuff."

"They're called 'deployments'. Don't get me wrong. A lot of couples make it work. I'm just saying that there are additional stressors in a military relationship than there are in relationships outside of the military."

"That makes sense. I can understand that."

Bobby reached a hand over and patted Sunny's knee. "If I make the choice to do the career thing, I'd want to be with somebody supportive but if I found the right person and had to give up the military, I'd do it in a heart beat." He brushed the back of his fingers on Sunny's cheeks.

"The right person would definitely be worth it," Bobby said in addition. He put his hands back onto the steering wheel and watched the traffic around them as he continued to drive.

Sunny was left to his own thoughts long enough to think things over and decide what all of these things that Bobby had told him meant to him and his own life. He needed to know it was possible. He didn't want the same thing that he currently had with Duke. He wanted different. He wanted better.

A tap on Sunny's knee brought him out of his reverie. He was brought back to the present. His present situation required him to produce his identification card so that they could proceed through the gate that they were at. The entrance to the airbase.

Sunny looked around and realized that he had been so distracted that he had failed to pay attention to the rest of their ride. He had missed when they had gotten off the freeway and drove up to the gate of the Airforce base. Sunny wondered about how long he had been distracted to have missed all of that. He wondered that Bobby had left him to drift in thought that entire time.

They drove through the gate and Sunny let those thoughts slip away. Bobby put them on a road that circled the airfield and Sunny found himself looking through a barbwire covered chainlink fence at the tarmac beyond. A row of very large aircraft grew larger still as they continued to drive around the airstrip. Bobby stopped the truck on the side of the road when they got as close as they could to the row of large airplanes.

Bobby got out of the truck and moved over to the chain linked fence. Sunny got out and joined him at the spot where he stood looking at the planes on the other side of the fence. They were the largest planes that Sunny had ever seen in his life.

"What are those?" Sunny asked Bobby.

"Those are C-5 Galaxies. They're the biggest cargo planes in the military."

"What can they carry?"

Bobby laughed. "They can carry a lot. They can carry the tanks that the Army uses."

"How heavy are those?"

"The tanks?" Bobby asked for clarification as Sunny nodded. "They're more than a few dozen tons each."

"Wow." Sunny turned from looking at the planes so that he could see Bobby. "You fly that thing?" He asked Bobby.

Booby let go of the fence and looked over at Sunny. He waved his hands in front of him.

"No, no. I'm not the captain. I'm just the first officer for that one there," said Bobby as he pointed at one of the planes out on the tarmac. "I'm usually the communications officer but our first officer is on sick leave so I'm filling in for him."

"So does that mean you'll never fly one of those?"

"Naw, it's gonna be a while before they let me fly that thing," said Bobby laughing easily. "Well, that's what I brought us up here for. To show you where I worked. Are you ready to go get something for lunch?"

Sunny nodded and they both went back to get into the truck. Bobby drove them off the base. He put them on the freeway heading south towards the city. He pulled them off of the freeway at one of the many midtown exits and found them a restaurant that they could stop and eat at.

SUNNY sat down with Bobby at the outdoor dining area, bathed in the golden glow of the setting sun. They had shared a day of laughter and connection, and the warm embrace of the sun seemed to mirror the warmth growing between them. As they talked about their dreams and desires, it was as if the sun's rays were illuminating their hearts, casting away any doubts and shadows. Each moment with Bobby felt like a sunlit adventure, promising a brighter future.

They soon ordered. Sunny was enjoying himself immensely and would have been satisfied with the time that they had already spent together that day. It was easy to be with Bobby and he felt like he really could be himself.

He didn't have to be anyone else but himself and that was fine by him. Who would want to have to go through life trying to be someone that they were not, when it was just so much easier to be yourself and if people didn't like the real you, then you could move away from them and gravitate towards the people that would accept you for who you were.

Bobby set his drink down and watched Sunny as he sat there people watching.

"So tell me about Sunny," Bobby eventually said.

"There's not much to tell. I work at a bank. I go to school online and I should be done with my journalism degree in a few months. And lastly, I love comedy."

"Why a journalism degree?"

"I've always liked being able to give people good news. I guess that came about because of the news I got about my mom's illness. I just think that there is too much emphasis on the bad news that's out there at the expense of the good things that happen. Somebody should be telling the stories about the good things."

"So how did it turn out that you ended up in comedy?"

Sunny laughed and said, "that's thanks to my best friend. I just had a knack of cheering people up some after they got some bad news. My best friend convinced me to give comedy a try. I did and I love it."

Bobby nodded and said, "your friend sounds really supportive. Its great to have friends like that. Everyone should have someone like that to support them."

"Yeah," said Sunny half heartedly. He reflected on how he and Miranda were not talking at the moment. He had caused that through is own actions. He realized he was going to have to find a way to bridge that gap that had grown up between him and Miranda. He loved her. He missed her. She was the Costello to his Abbott. She was the Yang to his Yin and he realized that more, now that they had this rift between them, than he had realized ever before in the past.

Bobby noticed the change in Sunny so he sought to shift the topic of their conversation to something else entirely. He had something that he wanted to address anyway, so he brought it up. "What's going on between you and... um...,"

"Duke?"

"Yeah. Him."

"I gotta let him go," said Sunny as he was shaking his head. "I can't be with someone like him anymore. It's just too much drama, plus, I have to deal with him denying being gay. It's just not worth the hassle anymore. I can do better."

"I'm glad you said that. I think you can do better as well."

Sunny stared at Bobby though narrowed eyes. "So what are you saying?" he finally asked Bobby. "Are you suggesting you can be that 'better' for me instead of Duke?" Sunny finished, half jokingly.

The seriousness of Bobby's expression half convinced Sunny that that was indeed the case. Sunny doubted it. He didn't know if he should take it as just talk or if he should take what Bobby was implying as a fact.

They had finished with their meal and Bobby had already paid. Only their drinks remained between them on the table. Sunny turned away from Bobby's intense stare and started messing with his glass.

"You're not serious, right?" asked Sunny.

He took a chance and looked up into Bobby's eyes. His intense gaze hadn't changed one bit in the ensuing time between his two questions.

A spark of fire ignited inside of his soul. He hoped. He longed. He wanted what was being implied to be true. Sunny averted his eyes.

"I still have to break things off with Duke," Sunny intoned softly.

Sunny didn't get a response from Bobby so he looked up into Bobby's eyes once more. He saw a smile, not only beginning to bud on Bobby's lips but also in his eyes. In the way that he sat. In the way that his muscular body moved.

"I'll wait," Bobby said enthusiastically.

"Why me?" asked Sunny evenly.

It was kind of hard to keep his voice steady. His heart had decided that it was no longer happy to be in the location that it had started in and so it had moved to a convenient enough place in his throat, where it could more easily threaten to cause him to choke up and start crying.

"You're just joking with me. You're not serious," Sunny rushed out.

He began moving around in his seat in preparation of standing up. Bobby quickly reached out his hand and covered Sunny's hand with his own. It was enough. The simple gesture caused Sunny to stop and remain still, while half standing. He wished fervently that he could quiet the thumping in his chest.

"I'm serious, and why you?" asked Bobby as he leaned to the side and looked as if he was trying to stare at the half standing Sunny's butt. "You've got cute cheeks."

Sunny stared at Bobby with a dumb look on his face. "What?"

"I'm joking," Bobby smiled. "Sit down."

Bobby waited for Sunny to sit back down so that they could continue talking. "I was joking about liking you because you've got cute cheeks."

Because Bobby had teased him a little bit ago, he decided to return the favor. "So I don't have cute cheeks then?" Sunny asked.

Sunny lifted up one side of his hips and looked down and around as if he could actually see his own butt while in the seated position that he was in. It was enough to break the small bit of tension that had crept in between them. Both men laughed with an ease and naturalness born from a mutual understanding of the same thing.

"Yes, you've got some great assets," Bobby joked. Both men laughed a little harder.

Bobby continued. "Why you? I think it's you because of who you are, Sunny. You're smart, you're funny, you're good looking and you're chasing your dreams. A lot of people are afraid to get out there and chase down their goals and dreams because they're scared of failure. I don't see that when I look at you."

"Are you talking about being in a serious relationship with a real future, Bobby? I don't think I could deal with what I'm going through with Duke anymore. I want more from life and more from an equal partner."

Bobby's response was to partially stand up so that he could lean across the table and kiss Sunny on the lips. Their kiss lingered for some moments before they finally broke apart. Sunny knew then what he wanted to do.

A few people walking by, along the sidewalk near to the outdoor dining area, saw the kiss between the two potential lovers. Two girls walking by caught Sunny's eye. Both girls hid their good natured smiles behind their hands and giggled. They sped off, linked arm in arm. Another couple that was nearby caught his eye next. It was a mixed couple. An asian guy with a black girl. The asian guy gave Sunny a thumbs up and they walked on past. This was as open a relationship that Sunny had ever hoped for.

"I'll wait for you because, in my heart, I think you're worth it," said Bobby as he sat back down.

A few people seated nearby heard Bobby say these words. Their small applause caused Sunny a momentary bit of embarrassment. They left the restaurant behind them shortly after that and carried out the good feelings that they both had received from the acceptance of them as a couple by the people that had responded kindly to their public display of affection.

Bobby took Sunny to a park where they walked around and enjoyed the warm and bright day. They held hands as they walked around. Sunny was enjoying every minute that they were getting to spend together. This was what he had always wanted from any relationship that he had ever been in since he had opened up to his sexual preference and started to openly date men. This was unlike anything that he had ever experienced before. The feeling was like lightning coursing through his blood.

Here was a wonderful man that wanted to be with him and was unapologetic about how open he was about wanting to be in a relationship with another man. This, above anything else that could have happened the rest of the time that they spent together, served to raise Bobby's worth in the eyes of Sunny.

The both of them stopped in the early evening in order to get something to eat for dinner. Bobby had insisted that they stop and get something to eat for dinner even though Sunny objected. He objected on the grounds that Bobby had already paid for the lunch that they had enjoyed and he had also paid for the coffee and ice cream that they had stopped for and enjoyed later on in the day. Sunny wanted to contribute some so that the entire outing would not have been funded by Bobby. He didn't want to be a financial burden to Bobby at the possible beginning of a relationship that was quickly promising to be everything that Sunny was looking for.

Bobby ignored all of the protests that Sunny presented to him. All of the arguments of why he should be allowed to at least pay for their dinner were ignored as if they were irrelevant to the situation at hand. Bobby easily derailed and dismissed Sunny's pleas and his continuously stated concerns, until Sunny ended up just finally deciding to let it go and accept things as they were.

After dinner, they drove around through the city streets before Bobby drove them both back to Sunny's house. He parked on the street in the front of the house and turned off the engine of his truck. They sat in silence for a minute before Bobby began speaking. "So, did you have fun today?"

Sunny looked over at Bobby and the smile blossomed on his face as he spoke to the man that he was beginning to really like. "I had the best time ever. I can't think of anything that could make the day any better."

"I can," said Bobby as he released the catch on his seatbelt.

He leaned across the space in the cab of the interior of the truck and captured Sunny's face in his hands. He turned Sunny to face him and pressed his lips against Sunny's own pliable and receptive lips. He broke the kiss when he settled back into his seat.

"Did that make the day any better?" asked Bobby.

"Perhaps," said Sunny slowly.

Sunny looked out of the passenger side window of the truck at his partially darkened home. He turned back towards Bobby.

"Do you want to come in?" Sunny asked.

Bobby smiled, "I thought you'd never ask."

Bobby and Sunny got out of the truck. Bobby locked it up and followed Sunny towards the front door of the house. He and Sunny walked hand in hand to the porch and they continued in this manner down the hallway to Sunny's room after they came through the front door. It was by a supreme effort of will that Sunny was able to keep his hands off of Bobby until they entered his room.

With the door securely closed behind them, Sunny was no longer obliged to have to keep his hands to himself. He quickly took advantage of this turn of events that led to the new situation where he was free to let his hands wander and explore the sculpted body standing there beside him.

Sunny started by taking Bobby's shirt off so that he could run his hands along the lines of his chest. Bobby was fit and he was cut. It was enough so that Sunny had to run his lips across that same skin that his hands had just skimmed across. He nibbled on Bobby's neck and once he was intoxicated enough by doing that, he moved down to the chest and bit softly there as well. Bobby had his hand behind Sunny's head and kept Sunny's lips pressed against his skin by not allowing Sunny to pull away from him.

Sunny's hands found where they wanted to rest. He kept them poised on Bobby's hips as he moved back up to kiss Bobby on his inviting, luscious lips. His hands traveled around so that Sunny was able to squeeze on Bobby's butt and get a vocal response from him. Bobby's moan crept out from around the kiss that was being shared between the two of them. Sunny's heart beat thudded against his chest and Sunny had a slight problem trying to catch his breath.

Sweat broke out on the skin of both men as they continued to work each other to higher states of arousal. Bobby had lost his pants some time in the minutes that they closed the door to the room to that moment that they were now in. Bobby helped Sunny to shed his clothes until they were both at a point where they could enjoy skin to skin contract. Only the air stood between them and this was quickly worked up into a heated state for the both of them.

Sunny's hand dropped down between Bobby's legs and he took a hold of him. His fingers brushed gently over the flesh, causing shivers to pass through Bobby. Sunny began to stroke back and forth with the tips of his fingers and Bobby buried his head into Sunny's shoulder.

Bobby eventually pushed Sunny back far enough where he could drop to his knees in front of Sunny. Sunny tried to protest but he was quickly silenced when Bobby took him into his mouth. Bobby worked his tongue around first. Sunny dropped his hands onto Bobby's shoulders. Bobby knew that he had Sunny then. He withdrew Sunny from his mouth and worked his saliva over the erect member with his hand.

Bobby worked quickly until he felt Sunny raise up onto his toes. At that point, Bobby removed his hand off of Sunny and put him back into his mouth. He worked the long, hard member with his intense desire to have Sunny erupt. He didn't have to wait too long before he had achieved the results that he was working towards. Bobby gulped and his throat convulsed until Sunny was done. Bobby then stood up and took the opportunity to turn Sunny around. He came up close behind Sunny and started kissing on Sunny's neck.

Sunny was building up. The heat of the body behind him had him boiling over. He wanted to be joined together with Bobby. He wanted to feel Bobby inside of him. He pushed back with his hips into Bobby's crotch and felt the hardness of him slip between his ass cheeks. Sunny reached behind him and grabbed a hold of Bobby, where he could, so that he could pull him closer while he grinned against him.

Bobby walked Sunny forward until Sunny could lean over the bed. When Sunny was steady enough, he placed himself into position and slowly pushed until Sunny grunted and he was in. Sunny didn't wait for Bobby, but instead, he started rocking back and forth until Bobby reached his own orgasm and released while still inside of Sunny. Bobby withdrew from Sunny and collapsed on the bed. Sunny went to his bathroom and got a wet towel and cleaned up. He brought out a fresh one for Bobby to use for that same purpose. When they were done, they curled up on Sunny's bed and fell asleep in one another's arms.

9

Sunny awoke in the morning enough that he became aware that he was not in bed alone. He also realized that he was wrapped up in someone else's arms. He was comfortable. He felt safe and secure. He was content enough to exhale his sigh that claimed his mood. This was what he wanted from a relationship. He wanted to hold someone and be held. He wanted to be together. Sunny knew that this was the place that he was meant to be. The place that he had always been searching for. Here, in these strong and steady arms, Sunny could find love and acceptance to end the drought that had always been on his horizon. Killing the land of 'hope' that he had continued, over the years, to fertilize and moving him to where he could dare to dream of the realization of his dreams.

Sunny rolled over in Bobby's arms. At first he was fine with just drifting back off to sleep in that loving embrace but he changed his mind. He wanted to see that sleeping face and wonder how he had gotten so lucky to find a man like Bobby. Sunny lay still in Bobby's enclosing arms. He watched as Bobby slept peacefully. His lips looked inviting. They were thick and partly open. Bobby's steady respirations caused his chest to rise and fall gently. The object of Sunny's intense scrutiny smiled slowly.

"Are you gonna just keep staring or are you gonna kiss me?" asked Bobby.

"I thought you were still asleep," said Sunny.

"I was," said Bobby. He opened his eyes so that he could take in the view of the man in his arms. "I woke up when you rolled over."

Bobby leaned forward and greeted his lover with a passionate morning kiss. The only reason that Bobby broke the kiss with Sunny was because his stomach rumbled rather loudly. Both of them laughed because of the sound.

"I guess you're hungry," said Sunny.

Bobby nodded in the affirmative. "I guess I could stand to eat something."

Sunny dis-entangled himself from Bobby's arms and sought to sit up. Bobby pulled him back down and stole another kiss from him before he finally let up and allowed Sunny to rise up off of the bed.

"Okay, sir," began Sunny jovially. "Let's see about getting something to eat."

Bobby's eyebrows arched up. "Are you cooking, sir?"

"I just might," said Sunny as he looked over his shoulder back at Bobby who was still in bed. "For you, I think I can do that."

Sunny pulled on his boxers and a t-shirt. Bobby got up out of bed and pulled on his boxer briefs and a shirt that had been proffered by Sunny. He slipped on the dress shirt and left it unbuttoned as he followed Sunny out of his room.

Sunny led the way for them towards the kitchen. His focus was on the sexy man that was walking closely behind him so he didn't notice the smell of eggs and bacon already being cooked. If he had noticed, then he would have suggested to Bobby that they leave to go and get something for breakfast away from there instead of him cooking them something for breakfast at the house.

As things were, he came out of the hallway and in view of the kitchen and stopped short when he saw his father in the kitchen, standing before the stove and cooking. Peter looked over from what he was doing. He saw his son and a smile began on his face. That smile faded slowly from his face when he saw Bobby. Bobby was not expecting Sunny to stop so suddenly, so he ended up not being able to stop in time to keep from bumping into Sunny.

Bobby looked around the still form of Sunny that stood planted in the hallway like a stone statue. Bobby knew that he hadn't run into granite but it felt that way for how stiffly Sunny was standing there. Bobby saw Sunny's father and proffered him a smile as he spoke to him.

"Good morning," said Bobby as he raised his hand up in greeting.

Peter looked at Bobby. He looked at what Bobby was wearing and then he looked at his son, whose face was drained of color. He turned back to the stove and devoted his attention to the pan that he had a death grip on.

"Coffee is in the pot. Get the mugs and set places on the table," said Peter in a monotonous tone, devoid of any real life or emotion.

The feeling in the room was not tense but it was not easy and open. It was with an effort that Sunny moved over to the cupboards and pulled down three plates. He handed these to Bobby and gave him instructions to set the table while he retrieved three mugs and the silverware that they would need to eat their meal. Sunny poured the three cups of coffee and put the carafe back. He hesitated at the counter before deciding that it would likely be a better idea to wait at the table instead of offering to help his father finish cooking the meal.

Peter came over and put bacon and eggs on all three plates. He went back and stopped at the stove so that he could get the tray of pancakes that he had also made. He gave everyone a portion and sat down with his son and Bobby so that they could eat.

They ate in silence at first. Sunny sat staring at his plate. Peter nursed his coffee cup. Bobby stared between the two of them and felt awkward in the space.

Bobby had no idea what he could do to help ease the tension but he was determined that he was not going to just sit there and do nothing in the uncomfortable space cause by the tense silence. He figured that he could start by introducing himself to Sunny's father first and then go on from there, assess the atmosphere, and decide on his next course of action.

"Hi, I'm Bobby," he said while addressing Peter.

Peter looked up from his coffee mug and stared blankly at Bobby. From Peter's reaction, it seemed as if he hadn't heard what Bobby had said at all. It was as if Bobby had spoken into the silence and interrupted Peter's train of thought. Peter blinked and came back to himself.

"Oh, yeah. Hi, I'm Peter, Sunny's dad. It's nice to meet you," said Peter unenthusiastically.

Bobby and Peter shook hands.

"Thanks for breakfast," said Bobby.

Peter didn't speak for a few minutes. He had picked his coffee mug back up after shaking hands with Bobby and now he had it poised at his lips as if he meant to take a sip. He put the coffee cup back down on the flat surface of the dining room table. He laced his fingers together and leaned back in his chair.

"Did you spend the night here last night?" he asked Bobby bluntly; no preamble used whatsoever.

Bobby's mouth dropped open. Sunny felt a sinking feeling in the pit of his stomach and hurriedly looked up at his father who just continued to sit there, waiting patiently for Bobby to answer him. Bobby could not understand why he suddenly got the feeling that he didn't want to answer the question, but he did answer anyway.

"Yes, I did," Bobby said hesitantly. "Is that a problem?"

Peter answered the question with a question of his own as he chose not to give a proper response. "Did you two have sex last night?"

Now Bobby was very certain that he didn't want to answer any questions. He didn't think that it would profit him in anyway with giving a response to Peter's question. Luckily for Bobby, Sunny jumped into the middle of the conversation and answered the question for Bobby instead.

"And if we did, is that a problem?" Sunny asked.

Peter looked over at his son and said, "I was talking to Bobby but since you asked, yes I have a problem with that."

"Wow," said Sunny. His head rolled back until he was staring at the ceiling. He dropped his eyes back onto his father.

"We did have sex last night, dad. So what now?" asked Sunny defiantly.

Peter leaned forward across the table towards his disrespectful son and said "I will not have the type of behavior under my roof. You will —,"

"I will what, dad?" asked Sunny, cutting off his dad. "You don't want gay sex in your house, is that it?" Sunny demanded.

"That's not what I'm...," Peter began but Sunny cut him off again so that he could not completely communicate what it was that he had wanted to say.

"I get it, dad. You don't want a gay son. You've made that pretty clear. You won't have to worry about me having sex with men under your roof again," Sunny stated with his voice rising in tone until he finally decided to get up from the table in preparation of leaving his father's presence. "I'll be moving out by the end of the week."

Sunny's words hung in the air, heavy with unresolved tension, like storm clouds gathering on the horizon. As he stormed off to his room, the atmosphere seemed to mirror his inner turmoil, much like passing clouds that temporarily obscure the brilliance of the sun. Peter watched his son's departure, his mouth opening and closing as he tried to find the right words to mend the rift he had inadvertently caused. Yet, like the sun struggling to break through a cloudy sky, he found nothing really appropriate to say that could ease the situation. He turned back to the table and looked down at his coffee cup, a symbol of the quiet discomfort that lingered in the room.

Peter watched his son storm out of the kitchen. His mouth opened and closed as he tried to work something out to say. Finding nothing really appropriate to say in the situation to make things better, he turned back to the table and looked down at his coffee cup.

Bobby didn't know what to do so he just continued to sit there in stunned silence. It was not until Sunny came back into the kitchen, moments later and fully dressed, that he finally decided that it was probably best if he got dressed as well and left. This was a family dynamic that he understood as best being handled, and potentially — hopefully resolved, without him being present in the midst of it. He stood up to leave the kitchen just as Sunny began to speak.

"I'm sorry about... this," said Sunny as he waved his hand in the air at the kitchen as a means to indicate the scene that had just played out during their breakfast. "I can't be here right now. I've gotta go."

Tears started to build up in the corners of Sunny's eyes. He looked away, just in case the dam burst and the tears began flowing more freely.

"Look, I'll call you later," he finally said to Bobby before turning and fleeing from the emotionally charged room.

Bobby watched Sunny as he left. He wanted to go to him. He wanted to comfort him but it was very apparent that those were two things that Sunny was not willing to stick around for. Bobby decided to hurry up and get dressed to see if he could catch up to Sunny before it was too late and he was gone.

"Excuse me," Bobby said to Peter as he left the table.

Bobby was around the corner too quickly to catch Peter waving him off. By the time that Bobby had gotten dressed and out of the front door to the house, Sunny had already driven off, leaving Bobby, and his trauma, behind in his wake. Bobby didn't think it was very considerate of Sunny to just leave him like that. He tried to call his cell phone but he got no answer.

Since Sunny was not responding and he could not — would not, stay where he was, he decided that it would likely be a rather good idea for him to leave and wait for Sunny to contact him later on when he had finally had a chance to process what had happened between he and his father. When Sunny had found a way to come to terms with what had occurred. If Sunny needed him, he was going to be there for him. He would make himself available.

Bobby was upset that Sunny had left without affording him the chance to try and console him, but he felt that the issue was not as urgent as being available to Sunny if he was needed. He knew that they would be able to reconcile the issue at a later time, after things had calmed down sufficiently for Sunny to deal with it.

AS for Sunny, he was hurt and confused. He was angry as well. His knuckles were brighter than the rest of the skin on his fingers. He released his death grip on the steering wheel and took a deep breath. He knew that he had acted hastily and that realization only served as the necessary fuel to anger his even further. He was mad because of what had transpired between him and his father. He was also mad because he had run out of the house, and in his haste to get away from his father and the situation, he had left Bobby behind.

When Sunny finally figured out what he did he then started to get the phone calls and text messages from Bobby. He chose to ignore them for two reasons. The first reason was because he was driving and angry and didn't need the added distraction of trying to talk on the phone while he was driving. The second reason was because he could not think of what he would say to Bobby about leaving him at the house like that while he bailed out alone. He had no idea now how to face Bobby now. He was embarrassed at his behavior and what his father had said.

Something else that Sunny had no idea of was where he was even actually going to. He had wanted to be away from his home, his father, and their argument, but that in no way meant that he knew where he wanted to be away *to*. He looked out of the windshield at the street just beyond that clear barrier of glass.

The sun was already up its rays slicing through the clouds of confusion in Sunny's mind. It had gotten up on time and did it's job. Because of that, Sunny could see where it was that he had gotten to so far. He had assumed that he had just been driving randomly — aimlessly, with no real destination in mind. That would have made sense because of his troubled state of mind, but that was actually *not* the case at all. Sunny easily recognized where he was driving to because he had done the drive so many times before in the past.

Sunny understood that he was not just running away from something, he was actually running towards something. Towards someone. He was running to where he knew his heart could be taken to start mending itself. The only problem with the current destination that he was heading to was the fact that he and Miranda had yet to discuss what had happened between them and resolve those issues.

Sunny wanted somebody to talk to. A shoulder to lean on and perhaps, maybe even to cry on. Sunny needed someone. He was not going to go to Duke. That was out of the question. He was reluctant to call on Bobby, even though he was sure that Bobby would be there for him if he needed it. He didn't want to go to Bobby because he felt that it was too much too early in their relationship to do that. Too early for him to depend on Bobby like that. This left him with little choice but to continue on to Miranda. She was the best choice that he had at the time anyway. She knew him better than anyone else and it was high time that they put the matter between them to rest. Once and for all. For both of their sakes.

Talking up the courage to do something you are not sure you want to do is one thing separate from actually doing the task. Sunny had hyped himself up to be ready for whatever outcome came his way with this situation that he had with Miranda. He failed to commit to the deed of going and knocking on her front door which could be the first step necessary, at this point, for he and Miranda to start mending broken fences.

Sunny took a deep breath and let it out. If the sun could get up everyday and do it's job, nonstop, then he felt he should be able to get out of his car, walk up those stairs, and go and knock on his best friend's door and present himself to her for an overdue apology. Sunny looked at the interior door handle of his car and decided he would take a few more deep breaths before he really committed himself and executed his plan. He had just inhaled his first breath when his phone went off and caused him to jump with a start. He looked at the caller identification on the phone and saw, to his surprise, that it was Miranda calling him. He answered on the third ring.

"Hello," Sunny answered hesitantly.

A brief silence ensued that made Sunny wonder, momentarily, if he had missed the call from Miranda. It lasted only a second before she spoke with her soft voice. "Are you gonna sit there all day or are you gonna come on up? I started some coffee."

Sunny could not help but to smile. The way they fell back into their comfortable routine was a testament to the strength and power of their friendship. There was an ease and a love there that Sunny could not help but to cherish. There was so much more to them than what could just be seen on the surface and because of that, it seemed that there could be nothing that ever came between them that would rend their friendship. Nothing would sever their kinship. Sunny felt pretty sure that his new insight into his friendship with Miranda was just one of those truths about the world — like the sun rising in the east — that would never change, no matter what.

He finally got out of his car. Despite the reason that had originally brought him to Miranda's place, he now wore a smile on his face. He had to chalk that up to the love that he felt for the crazy girl that he was about to go and see. The upcoming makeup was beginning to feel like a homecoming of sorts and he was now more keenly aware of just how much he was ready to get back into the swing of things with Miranda.

Once Sunny finally got up the stairs, he found the door was unlocked and partially open, so he was able to just walk on into the apartment. He was not surprised when a blur of a little black girl raced towards him and jumped up into his arms. She clung to Sunny's neck and it took an extreme amount of balance, on Sunny's part, to keep them from falling over with her draped all over him. He didn't mind at all. Even when he felt her tears soaking his shirt, he didn't mind. His own tears were freely flowing into her hair.

"I'm sorry, Miranda."

Miranda sniffed. Her small fists pummeled Sunny's back. "You made me cry, you jerk."

"Let me dry your eyes," said Sunny as he slowly peeled Miranda off of him like a stubborn bandage.

"I'm talking about *that* day *and* today."

Sunny stopped pulling away from Miranda and instead crushed her close to his chest. He felt the shudder passing through her small body as she tried to suppress her crying. "I wasn't aware of how you felt. I should have seen it. I mean, we've been friends since forever and I can't believe I just didn't see it."

"I'm sorry too. It wasn't fair to you to not let you know. There were a lot of times when I could've just said something, but I didn't."

Sunny kissed her on the forehead and was able to finally maneuver the both of them over to the couch so that they could sit down. "So talk to me, Miranda. Tell me about your feelings."

Miranda kicked her feet up on the couch and laid out on Sunny. She made herself as comfortable as she could. She wrapped Sunny's arm around her waist and smiled up at him as she started telling him, from the beginning, what she should have let her best friend know years ago. She would talk about it now because she had to. It was time to let the captured bird out of its cage so that it could grow and live however nature intended for it to live.

"When I first met you, I didn't know that you were gay until you told me. The only reason that I started bugging you was because I had a major crush on you. When I found out that you were gay, I had to find a way to deal with it."

"I don't understand. I know everything about you. I can't believe that I missed something that huge," Sunny admitted. His hands rubbed his forehead as he shook his head back and forth.

"You were the only one that couldn't see it," said Miranda with a laugh. "Just about everyone else could see that I had a thing for you. I was able to move on, but I wasn't able to completely stop loving you like that."

"Well, I should've known it. You mean the world to me, Miranda, and I mean that."

"Yeah, okay. I know you're 'strictly dickly' and I wasn't trying to change that. I just couldn't help myself right then and I had to kiss you. You don't have to worry about me doing that again," said Miranda.

Miranda turned away from him as she finished speaking. Sunny touched her cheek and turned Miranda to face him. When she was turned towards him, he leaned down and kissed her on the lips. The kiss lingered a lot longer than a friendship kiss would have. He slipped his tongue into her mouth and felt her shudder as her eyes fluttered closed. Sunny pulled away slowly when he felt the kiss had lasted long enough. Miranda gasped.

"I'm sorry. I can't give you more than that, sweetie," said Sunny softly.

Miranda reached up with her arms and pulled Sunny back to her lips for a quick and gentle kiss. "It was enough, boo. Thank you."

Miranda got up and went into her galley kitchen. She returned with two mugs of coffee and gave one to Sunny. She sat back down next to Sunny and leaned over into his waiting embrace.

"So, what brought you over?" she asked.

"How did you know I was here for a problem?" Sunny asked her seriously.

Miranda looked over her shoulder into Sunny's eyes. She gave him a wry smile with one corner of her mouth twisted up.

"Oh, I get it. You can read me like a book," said Sunny.

"You got it, buster," said Miranda jokingly. "So what's on your mind?"

"My dad and his attitude. I want to move out. I told him I'd be out of his house by Friday."

"Well if you need somewhere to go, somewhere to stay...go find another friend," Miranda laughed as she watched the look on Sunny's face turn to hurt. "I've got only one bedroom," she explained.

"You've got this awesome couch."

"Yeah, it's for *sitting*, not *sleeping*."

"I thought we were friends."

'We *are*, that's why I'm asking what happened."

Sunny sighed. He decided to approach staying with her at a later time. He decided, instead, to open up about what happened recently. "Duke and I were at the club on Friday and your Bae showed up. Apparently he had just robbed Duke. Duke pistol whipped him in the parking lot and drove off in Black Vic's car. Duke wanted me to leave with him, but I didn't. I don't want that stuff in my life. The cops are probably still looking for him now, or not. I don't know if your Bae pressed charges. I think I'm going to give up on Duke."

Miranda took a sip of her coffee and put the mug on the table that was positioned next to the couch. She turned sideways and leaned back into Sunny. He wrapped his arm around her again and pulled her closer. She felt safe in those arms and didn't want to ever be the cause of losing the ability to be in them.

"I think I owe you an apology, Sunny," Miranda said slowly.

"Why?"

"Victorious was over here on Saturday and I let it slip that you and Duke were together."

Sunny kissed the top of Miranda's head yet again. "That's alright. I think he already figured it out anyway. He saw us together before that at Duke's house. That was when Duke denied that he was gay, remember."

"Wow, what an ass."

"Tell me about it."

"So what does that have to do with why you got into it with your dad?" asked Miranda as she looked over her shoulder again at Sunny.

"Nothing," Sunny replied quickly while trying to hide his smile.

Sunny was not going to be able to tell Miranda why he and his father had a disagreement without having to tell her about he and Bobby first. So he did. He told her everything that had happened after he met Bobby again on that Saturday night.

Miranda listened quietly while Sunny spoke. She offered or added the necessary cues that were customary and expected when being told something. She kept all of her questions close until she was certain that Sunny had definitely finished telling her his tale of a fated meeting of lovers. Miranda didn't move, other than snuggling up as closely as she could, until the last word that Sunny uttered fell away into silence.

Miranda had her coffee mug in her hands again. She had her lips pressed up against the brim and she spoke around that. "Sunny, he sounds amazing."

Sunny had to agree. He thought Bobby was a godsend as well. "I think so too," he confided to Miranda.

"Are you gonna start dating him?"

"I'd like to. I'm worried though. I also have to let Duke know that I'm moving on. I can't deal with being with a thug and drug dealer like him. It's more than I can handle."

"I can understand the stuff about Duke. I think you need to leave him too. I'm gonna leave Victorious alone too," Miranda said as she put down her coffee mug again. "Why are you worried though?"

"I don't want to scare Bobby away with this drama with Duke and the stuff with how my dad is acting lately."

"Yeah, that's a lot to deal with. I think you should take care of Duke though, before you do anything else."

Sunny was about to respond, but his phone started buzzing, giving him the notification that he had a text message that had just come in. He unlocked the phone and perused the message quickly. "Speak of the devil."

"What do you mean?" asked Miranda.

"Duke just texted me. He wants me to stop by."

Miranda sat up off of Sunny in a hurry. She turned to fully face him. "Are you gonna go and see him?"

"Do you think I should?"

"Yeah. So you can break it off with him."

"You're right. I just can't do that by text either," said Sunny as he kissed Miranda on the forehead and then finished off his coffee before he left to go and see Duke.

10

I ndistinct music rumbled through the speakers of the stereo. The volume was low so the actual words were a bit muffled. The volume of the stereo matched the low lights that struggled to illuminate the space inside of the house. The blinds were closed shut and were were dark curtains drawn to block out the light of day. Most mischievous activity was conducted in the dark and so were the actions in this room.

Two individuals sat in the living room, working in the dim light. They didn't speak to one another but instead, working in silence, they understood what needed to happen without resorting for verbal communication to make it happen. Just as the blinds remained closed, blocking out the sun's brilliance, their intentions were veiled, obscured from the light of day. Stale marijuana smoke was thick in the air, from wall to wall. The smell of the burning marijuana barely covered the smell of the cleaning solvent that was being liberally applied to the gun parts that were spread out by Echo on the short table.

Black Vic took the blunt that Echo passed to him and pressed it up against his lips so that he could inhale the intoxicating smoke. He winced in pain when the blunt touched his split lip. The beating that he had taken from Duke had left him with the split bottom lip that he nursed as carefully as he could. The beating also left him with a left eye that he could barely see through because of how swollen the eye was. The bruised eye was already blackened from the blood that had pooled beneath the skin around it.

It was a mixed miracle that he didn't have a broken nose or that both of his eyes had been hit, causing him to have two swollen eyes instead of just the one that he did have. It was a blessing that he didn't have any fractures to the bones of his face. Duke had struck him in the face enough with that pistol where that would have been a serious concern. His injuries would heal fine and barely leave much in the way of a scar, as long as he took care while letting his face heal. As things stood right then, that was the last thing that he was thinking of.

What could not be seen, but was suffering from the trauma just as bad as his physical well being, was his hurt ego. His shattered reputation. Both of these had suffered just as harshly as his physical self. Just as harshly by Duke's hands as his face had been injured. Black Vic felt powerless. Not weak, but still stripped of his strength. Anyone that now saw his face would also assume that Black Vic was weak and that was his main concern. Not powerless in those views, but unable to show strength because his strength hadn't been a factor in keeping him from receiving the beating from Duke.

How could Black Vic demand respect with his face looking like it did? He could not; not in his opinion. He was not going to inspire fear and get the respect that he felt that he deserved until he did something to redeem himself in the eyes of his soldiers and the other gangsters and thugs on the streets that he walked and drove through. This transgression was going to require that the payment price for redemption be fulfilled in blood. Black Vic wanted it to be Duke's blood and if he had his way he was going to make that happen. This was personal. Things were now lining up nicely for him so that he had that opportunity at his disposal to demand that reparation. All Black Vic had to do now was count to thirty. At thirty, he would be done filling up the magazine that he was putting rounds in. At thirty, he could start counting again as he loaded the next one.

Bingo came back into the dimly lit living room from the kitchen. He took a spot next to Black Vic on the couch and opened up the beer that he had in his hands. He took a very long swig from the bottle before he uprighted it again. He leaned back on the couch and watched Black Vic finish loading rounds into the second magazine that he had started loading. He was interested in how many rifles and guns they were going to be using shortly and wondered why they were taking so many along with them instead of just taking one or two and just reloading but he was not about to voice his concern to Black Vic. He knew that Black Vic was not in a good mood following what had occurred a few nights previously.

"We can call in some shooters. I know a couple young bulls dat wanna be put on, Black Vic. Ya heard? I don't think chu need to be involved in dis shit. Me and Echo can take care of dis shit. Ya heard?" said Bingo.

Black Vic didn't look over at Bingo. He kept loading the magazine until he was done and the magazine was full. He put it down and turned his attention to Bingo so he could address what he said. He wanted to make sure that Bingo understood him and his intentions with this issue he wanted to deal with.

"Nah, man. Dis shit here is personal. I got dis one," said Black Vic as he put the magazine down and gingerly touched his lip where the split had bled out a tiny little bit more. "I'mma air dat fool out and I don't care who dere. I'll smoke his moms. His pops. I don't give a fuck, as long as dat nigga dead."

Bingo leaned forward and picked up a part of a gun off of the table. He turned it over and around in his hand as he looked at it. Echo made a noise to get his attention. Echo held out his hand to take the upper receiver of the assault rifle from the hands of Bingo so that he could reassemble the rifle. Bingo passed off the part and picked up another off of the table. There were many mixed parts of guns and rifles on the table and Black Vic and Bingo depended on Echo to know how to clean them and reassemble them.

"What chu need me and Echo to do? Ya heard?" asked Bingo as he leaned back into the ratty couch that he and Black Vic were sitting on.

"I need for you to pass me dem poles from the back when I empty dem clips. I'm unloading every thang. Echo gone handle de whip. Is dat cool?"

"Yeah, whatever man, ya heard?" said Bingo sarcastically.

Black Vic looked over at Bingo. He hadn't liked how Bingo had just spoken to him at all. He was not in the mood to deal with anyone else's attitude but his own right then. He definitely was not willing to deal with it from one of his lieutenants.

"What da fuck dat s'ppose ta mean? You gotta problem, brah? Dere some'n' chu feel like saying, nigga?" Black Vic growled.

"It ain't like dat, Black Vic. I just thought I could dump on dat fool wit' chu. You know, open up on 'em with mo heat, ya heard?"

Black Vic calmed down a little bit. His temper had flared massively when he thought that Bingo had overstepped his bounds; stepped out of line and was being very disrespectful to him. He already had to deal with keeping his soldiers in line after what had happened between him and Duke got out on the streets. He didn't want to have one of his best lieutenants questioning him about his decisions. It had never happened in the past with his boys so he was not ready to deal with it, especially right now. The situation only served to anger him even further, the more that he was forced to remember the beating that he had received from Duke.

"Dis one is on me. I'mma do dis one on my own. I just need you to keep puttin' fresh heat in my hands," said Black Vic.

"You got it, Black Vic. Ya heard?" said Bingo.

Black Vic would have smiled but his split lip would not let him. It hurt too bad to do so and smiling would make his lip start bleeding yet again. He didn't want to deal with that. He had to settle for a malicious laugh filled with the venom that he wanted to spew all over Duke. His chance was coming up and Duke was going to see a retaliation for the beat down that he had parceled out on Black Vic. He was going to see a retaliation that he hoped would end his worries about Duke or either by killing him or seriously injure Duke. Black Vic's thoughts dwelled on his revenge and he was even willing to accept any casualties that might occur, as long as it impacted Duke in some way.

There was nothing that was going to turn Black Vic from the path that he had decided to travel. Nothing was going to be allowed to get in his way. If anything got into his way with this, then he was going to bowl it over and leave it destroyed behind him. He would mow it down in a hail of gunfire. The only thing that was in his sights, was seeing Duke's body getting riddled with bullets. That was going to make him happy. That was going to make things better. That was the way that he was going to resolve this issue that he had with Duke.

The pleasure that Black Vic felt in visualizing the culmination of his goal helped to motivate him to plan for further violence. He wanted to sit back and watch the world as it burned. He wanted to see the flames consume everything that he could see. There was nothing that he would not be happy seeing reduced to ashes as a result of being consumed by the flames. Why should he care for what happened to the world when he felt that the world had never cared for him. It didn't feed him when he was hungry as a child and it didn't give him a blanket with which to keep him warm on those cold nights that were spent inside of a house that was bereft of electricity or gas.

Everything that Black Vic had ever gotten he had to scratch and fight for. That was all that he knew. It was enough for him to survive. It was enough to help him get from one day to the next and do it all over again on that following day. He would put the rest of the world in the same darkness that he had always known his entire life. He would burn it all down to ashes and then sift through those ashes and take what he wanted and nothing was going to stop him. He would see to that. All that glittered, all that shimmered, all that shined, would be his and his alone. Not even Duke was going to be able to deny him what he wanted to take in life.

Black Vic picked up the rifle that Echo had reassembled. He loaded a magazine into the modified AR-15 and stared down the iron sights of the rifle. It was modified to be fully automatic. It was *highly* illegal but he didn't care one bit. It was just one of the half dozen weapons that he was planning on using. All the assault rifles were modified to be fully automatic. All of the assault rifles were illegal enough to put him, and everyone associated with them, in jail for a significant amount of time. He looked over at Echo and that malicious grin came to his face anyway, despite the pain caused by his split lip.

"Let's get da rest of deese put back together. I wanna be outta here in 'bout twenty or thirty minutes," said Black Vic.

Echo nodded and began putting the rest of the weapons back together. He handed them off to Bingo who loaded the right magazine into each rifle before he put them into the duffle bag that sat at his feet on the floor. Things were going to get dangerous in the near future as each of these weapons were used in the commission of a serious crime that would likely take a life at the end of their usage.

SUNNY shielded his eyes from the early blinding afternoon sun that hung up in the sky. He flipped down his visor and realized that it had been a pointless thing to do because his turn was coming up and that would put the sun on his right side and out of his eyes for the rest of the ride. He just ignored it and kept on driving. The visor was not hurting anything, and doing useless things like flipping down a visor that he was only going to need for a short amount of time made it easy for him to keep his mind off of what he was actually going to do. At least it kept him thinking about something else for a little while and that is what he felt like he really needed. He was letting the task that he was going to accomplish mill in the back of his mind. He let his present thoughts drown out the noise that was associated with what he was needing to do.

He wanted to be done. He wanted to be done with the games. He was ready to leave it all behind him and drive away from his numb feelings that swirled constantly around in his most recent thoughts of Duke. There was somewhere else that he knew he was now needed at. Wanted at. It was somewhere that he could be only himself, both behind closed doors and out in public. He was sure that he was going to hate having to breakup with Duke in person but that was just the type of person that he was. He was not the type of person to be lazy and cowardly enough to breakup with someone via a text message or a phone call. The person he broke up with might care less about the method being 'in person' but it ultimately allowed Sunny to at least feel good about himself and be able to look at himself in the mirror.

There was now someone better out there for him. It was not like he purposely went out and looked for someone else. Lord knew that when he was with someone, he was in through the thick and the thin, but the only way that attitude could work for him now was if he saw that his significant other, that was in the relationship, had the exact same mindset. With matching views of the world any couple could make it through the difficult times. Any couple could overcome the challenges that life threw at them. Any couple could beat the odds and come out on top of it all.

Sunny pulled up in front of Duke's house. He parked the car and sat inside of it while he tried to prepare himself, mentally, for the problems that might lay ahead of him when he eventually walked into Duke's house and told him that they were through. There were so many things that could happen while telling Duke that he no longer wanted to be with him that Sunny was not really sure of what things he could expect to happen. He wanted a clean break. He hoped that maybe things would be easy enough to end, after all. Maybe they would be able to have the clean break that would be best for both of them.

Nothing was going to happen at all if he didn't get started. He was going to have to eventually get out of his car, go and ring that doorbell, and bring all of these things to an end. Nothing would change for the better until he did those few things he thought he knew he ought to do to affect the changes that he wanted. Those things like 'getting out of the car, ringing the doorbell, and bringing things to an end'. Sunny took a deep breath, strapped some steel onto his backbone and got ready for the drama that was probably going to be part and parcel with breaking up with Duke.

Sunny got out of his car and stretched before he went to the front door of Duke's house. He knocked on the door instead of ringing the doorbell. It was answered more quickly than he was ready for so the expression on his face was one of surprise when Duke answered the door after only one knock. Sunny eyed Duke rather critically and decided that Duke didn't look too much for the worst, even though Sunny had let him drive off on his own and hadn't spoken to him, even once, since the night when all of that madness had happened.

Sunny gave a half hearted smile to Duke as he stood at the threshold of Duke's house waiting to be invited in, or at least spoken to with a cordial greeting of some kind. His wait was not long before it ended. Duke stepped to the side and gave Sunny the room that he needed to walk past him and enter the house. Duke closed the door after Sunny once he was past the threshold and inside of the house.

Sunny followed Duke into the living room. He took a seat on the all too familiar couch and got as comfortable as he could. He was still not as calm as he wished that he could have been. He was tense because of the situation and having to breakup with Duke. His stomach twisted into knots as Duke sat down on the couch beside him. It should have been easy for Sunny to tell Duke that he was going to move on. It should have been easy for Sunny to say what he needed and wanted to say because of all of the things that Duke had done so recently. It should have been easy because he had found Bobby. He had found the place where he believed he should be. Where he should have been from the beginning.

Duke still looked good. Sunny had to admit to that. He had to admit that much to himself. The man was a big bundle of chocolate goodness. If he was a candy bar, Sunny would enjoy unwrapping him and eating him all up, over and over again. Those thoughts flitted through Sunny's mind. They only served to distract Sunny from what he had come to Duke's house to discuss with him. He didn't need those thoughts distracting him or maybe even dispelling him from his ultimate goal. There was no need for that and Sunny was certain that moving on from Duke was definitely in his best interest.

Every time that a thought of Duke potentially derailed his ambition, he forced himself to think of the kind of gentle man that loved him for who he was and who was waiting patiently for him. Duke reached over to put his hand on Sunny's knee. Sunny moved his leg subtly so that Duke's hand missed landing where he had intended it to land and instead, Duke ended up with his hand planted on the couch between the two of them. Duke was not discouraged. He leaned over to try and kiss Sunny. Sunny turned away from the kiss.

Sunny would have stood up and moved somewhere else in the room, outside of Duke's reach, if Duke had continued to initiate intimate contact but he didn't have to. When Sunny turned away from Duke's attempt at a kiss, it gave Duke all of the signal that he needed. He got enough information from both gestures by Sunny. The message was communicated that his touch was unwanted. It was loud and clearly displayed.

"What's good, brah?" asked Duke with some frustration in his voice.

Sunny didn't answer, he just sat beside Duke and continued to stare at him.

Duke shook his head and asked, "chu still bent over dat shit dat went down?"

Sunny continued not to respond to Duke. He held his silence while only looking at him. Duke stood up and stalked off. His hands were clenched and then they unclenched and he repeated the action several times.

"What's goin' on? Why you actin' like dis?" he asked Sunny.

Sunny was stunned. He could not believe that Duke had asked that question of him and was acting as if Sunny should be fine after he witnessed Duke behaving so violently. It seemed to Sunny that the reason for his mood should have been obvious but apparently it was not the case. Duke apparently needed Sunny to break it down into the simplest terms that he possibly could for Duke so that there would be minimal, to no chance, of a misunderstanding of what he was trying to communicate.

"I think it would be best if we stopped seeing each other, Duke."

Duke stopped pacing and looked over at Sunny. The look on his face was one of astonishment. "What da hell chu thought dis was? Chu thought chu was my *bitch* or somethin'? Nigga, chu was just a hole fo' me to put my big ass *dick* in."

"Are you kidding right now?" asked Sunny. "Is this a joke?"

"Chu tell me, brah. I never said I was wit chu like that. You got me twisted or confused with some otha nigga look like me. I'm a real man."

"So I'm *not* a real man because I sucked your dick and let you fuck me? Get real, Duke. You're just too scared to admit that you're gay and face the truth of it."

Duke rushed Sunny. He stood close by where Sunny was sitting on the couch. He stood, towering over Sunny, trying to intimidate him into backing down with his presence over him. "What da fuck chu say, bitch?"

Sunny looked at Duke's fists as they clenched and opened. He looked up into Duke's eyes. He saw anger there. It blazed like a roaring flame that his soul should could not contain. Duke's eyes shone with a sheen that could have been caused by smoke irritated eyes, but it was the enclosed and encapsulated fury that caused it. Sunny also saw that there was something else buried deep in Duke that could be barely seen in the depthless pools of his eyes. Sunny squinted so that he could get a better look into the eyes of the angry man standing in front of him. What Sunny was looking to identify was hanging out right there at the corner of Duke's eyes. It hovered right there at the edge of the tears that refused to fall. Sunny was finally able to identify what it was that he was oh so easily able to see; like he could see no time before. It was fear.

"Are you scared, Duke?"

"What da hell I gotta be scared of?"

"Are you scared of being gay? Scared to say you like men?"

"I ain't no punk!" Duke declared fervently.

"What do you think it means to want to have sex with me if you're a man? You are *gay* Duke."

Duke inched forward as far as he could. "Say it again 'n see what happen."

Sunny narrowed his eyes again and set his jaw. He sat up straight so that he was slouching no more. "You like having sex with men. That makes you gay."

Sunny had no sooner finished his statement before he felt Duke's fist close in on his jaw and strike him solidly. The unexpected punch caught him partially off guard and caused him to tumble to the ground, falling off of the couch and dropping quickly. He came up on one knee and with one hand on the floor supporting him. His other hand was closed around his jaw and he looked up defiantly at Duke. Duke took a step back involuntarily. It was the look in Sunny's eyes that had made him step back. There was a something in his fierce gaze that Duke had never seen before. It told him to back off quickly.

"Are you done, Duke?" Sunny asked. He waited for a reply. When no reply was evidently to be had, he said, "If you're done now, so am I. Are you done, because if you're not, I'm gonna kick your narrow ass up and down the hallway of your own house. So...*are you done*?"

Duke another step backwards. Unlike the hesitant halfstep back that he had taken earlier, this one was a full blown, six inch step backwards. He was in full retreat; at least for that one step.

"I thought so," said Sunny. He reached a hand behind him to the couch. He used the couch as support as he stood up. Sunny still had one hand to his face. He used the hand on his face to rub his chin and take some of the sting out of the blow that had put him on the floor.

Duke stumbled forward to try and help the unsteady Sunny back to his feet. He reached out, only to have his outstretched, helping hand, smacked away in disgust.

"Don't!" hissed Sunny. "Don't fucking *touch* me."

Duke backed away again. He kept playing this dancing game where his body would automatically jerk forward because of his thoughts that propelled him forward, wanting to be of assistance to Sunny. He would abruptly stop when he remembered how his hands were batted away when he went to help Sunny stand up earlier.

"I'm…I'm sorry," stammered Duke.

Sunny stopped moving and looked at Duke in astonishment again.

"I din't mean dat, brah. Let's just talk 'bout it," Duke pled.

"Are you *crazy*? You think I have so little respect for myself that I'm gonna sit here and listen to anything that you have to say after you put your hands on me? You got me all kinds of fucked up. You better be glad that I don't fuck you up right now, Duke."

Duke came forward again with outstretched arms. "Please, let's—," he began.

Sunny cut him off with a raised hand. "There is nothing that you are going to be able to say to me now…or ever, that's gonna make me want to listen to anything you've got to say."

"That was done without thinking. I mean I was heated, brah."

Sunny just continued to stare at Duke. The look eventually made Duke fall quiet. "You need to move out of my way, Duke. I need you to move because I'm about to leave here, right now, and I'm never coming back."

"You ain't got to go nowhere. C'mon, brah. Sit back down and let's talk 'bout dis," Duke began pleading in earnest.

Duke tried to approach Sunny again but was quick to stop when he saw Sunny pull back away from him. As things stood, he was beginning to see — know, the truth of things. He had finally pushed too much and it was no longer a possibility that he was going to lose Sunny; it was a full blown certainty.

It was a certainty that if he let Sunny leave, he was definitely never coming back. When Sunny walked out of his front door, Sunny was going to walk out of his life forever. There was no recovering from this for Duke. This relationship had ended. It had reached the end of it's short life expectancy. Nothing that he did was going to be able to extend the life of that relationship. He had pushed Sunny away with his own actions. When the realization finally hit Duke that he and Sunny were done, he got angry.

"Well, if it's like dat den, get the fuck on. Take yo bitch ass out my house, nigga," spewed Duke.

Sunny looked at Duke in stupefaction. He was really at a loss for words to say in response to the ignorance that Duke was spewing. His mouth worked convulsively as he tried to work out what to say.

"You are one hell of a piece of work, you—," began Sunny before all hell broke loose all around him.

SUNNY was interrupted by the sound of gunfire. The sound of gunfire coming from outside of Duke's house. Bullets began shredding the room around Sunny as they tore through the facade of the house. Each single round, followed closely by another successive round, served as the one point of destruction that blew through wood, glass and plaster while making a path open up before it. The material that was used in the construction of the house became as much of a hazard as the bullets that tore through the house. Broken glass and flying splinters of wood sprayed everywhere in the space, adding to the chaos.

Duke was on the floor, with his head covered by his arm, in attempt to keep debris from hitting him in the face. He looked up once, just long enough to find out where Sunny was and what he was doing. He spotted Sunny and came up just high enough to grab a hold of Sunny and pull him down to the floor and away from the hail of bullets that were pouring into, and through, the house at the height at which Sunny had been standing. Duke pushed Sunny's head down to the floor and he admonished him to stay down and out of the path of the projectiles that were buzzing past, just above both of their ducked heads.

"Stay put and don't move!" Duke screamed.

He need not have said the last two words to Sunny. Sunny had no plans of moving while bullets decided that the route that they wanted to take, when exiting the guns that were firing them, was right above his head. He was very sure that he didn't want to play dodge ball with bullets. That just didn't seem to Sunny to be one of those smart things to do at the moment.

He decided that he didn't want to put on a mitt and try playing catch with something moving so damn fast. He was going to do exactly what Duke told him to do; he was going to stay plastered to the floor like a throw rug and keep his ass still so that he didn't accidentally bump into one of those damn bullets that were throwing temper tantrums in the house.

Sunny was terrified but when he looked over at Duke, he saw a man who was determined to keep him alive. Duke was partially covering Sunny with his own body. While it was a testament to how much Duke wanted to protect Sunny, it was ultimately a futile effort in the end. When all things were considered and balanced, Duke still came up holding a deficit. It was a huge deficit that could possibly cost Sunny his life.

Sunny was certain, without a shadow of a doubt, that Duke's lifestyle was the preliminary impetus that had been necessary to precipitate this shower of bullets, shards of glass, chunks of wall plaster, and splinters of wood. That was the first mark that put Duke into the hole and owing. The second thing that compounded the deficit was the fact that at the rate that the bullets were entering the house, there was no certainty of either of the two men remaining free of those pesky bullet holes that were appearing all around both of them while they hugged the floor.

The nail in the coffin, as far as Sunny could determine, was that one of those damn bullets could easily pass through Duke's flesh and still strike him dead, even with Duke trying to shield him with his own body. Sunny stopped being terrified and downgraded to just scared. He was able to do that because he had also shifted up a gear, on another level, and at the same time became exceedingly pissed at Duke.

Duke moved off from over Sunny. Sunny watched him move carefully across the room, while staying as close as he could to the floor and out of the path of the hail of bullets traipsing through the house and colliding with the far wall of the room that they were in. Amid the chaos, the room was lit by intermittent streams of sunlight that filtered through bullet-riddled walls. As Duke kept moving across the floor to the window — or what remained of the window — in the front of the house, Sunny noticed something in his hand. It was the biggest revolver that Sunny had ever seen in his life. The barrel alone looked like it was about eight to ten inches long. Sunny was wondering what Duke was trying to do or what plan he was coming up with by getting closer to the front of the house and then it slowly dawned on him. Duke was going to return their fire. Sunny thought that it was a stupid idea. It was chaos in the house with those bullets zipping back and forth everywhere.

Sunny was sure that when Duke stuck his head up to shoot back that he would end up catching a bullet or two. Maybe even three. At that point, Sunny really thought that Duke was stupid. However, when Sunny actually started paying attention to what was going on, he noticed that there were lulls in the rate of fire coming into the house. Sunny assumed that the shooter was reloading and he ultimately realized that Duke was smart enough that he had noticed this too and was waiting on one of these periods, that were free of gunfire, to pop up and then shoot back at the gunman that was outside the house.

It was not long before another one of those breaks occurred. In the silence, Sunny watched as Duke came up. He level the gun at something outside of the house, and beyond Sunny's line of sight. Duke had both hands wrapped around the handle of the revolver and Sunny wondered briefly if that was actually necessary. He was not well versed on guns. The only real experience that he had with them came from watching them being employed — to various effects — on television. Because of his naivety, he was unprepared for the sound when the handgun was finally fired. He saw the gun kick back violently in Duke's hands while at the same time, it sounded like a clap of thunder sounded off within the confines of what was left of the living room of the house.

Sunny determined that Duke had set off a medieval cannon; that it could not have been a modern firearm that he had just used. The sound seemed to echo incessantly between his ears, even though he had clamped his hands over his ears. It was not until a few minutes later that Sunny realized that it was not echoes of the gun firing that he was hearing. It was Duke continuously pulling on the trigger of that hand cannon after reacquiring his target in his sights. Whatever it was that Sunny witnessed Duke doing with that big ass gun must have had the desired effect because Sunny noted that the house was not getting ventilated and aired out anymore. Sunny was also aware of the sound of an engine revving up and tires squealing as some vehicle outside sped off in the distance.

Sunny let out a breath that he didn't know that he had been holding. He reached up to his forehead and wiped away some of the debris that had landed on him during the assault. It felt to Sunny like his hand was slick with sweat as he wiped across his forehead. He pulled his hand in front of him and stared at it like an idiot. He was not sure of what he was looking at. It seemed familiar and that he should know what was covering his hand but he could not seem to think of the word for it. Duke looked back at Sunny and Sunny turned his attention to him as. Duke called out to him.

"Is you okay...," he began questioning before he stopped talking and really paid attention to Sunny.

He looked at Sunny's hand. The hand that Sunny was holding in front of him. Sunny's face and his hand were wet with blood. The front of his shirt was covered in blood and it was continuously spreading out and soaking the shirt as Duke continued to look at Sunny.

Sunny felt his chest getting tighter and it felt like he had a stack of two hundred bricks pressing on his chest. Sunny looked at his chest and saw a small dark hole pumping out frothy blood from the right of his chest. When he looked back up, he noticed that Duke had closed all of the distance that had been between them in what seemed like less than a second. He thought that he heard Duke say something to him but he could not really make out what he was saying. Sunny looked into Duke's eyes and gave him an angry smirk. He was pissed then.

"Like I was saying. You are one hell of a piece of work..., you ass," Sunny wheezed through the pain in his chest.

Duke caught Sunny in his arms as he collapsed into a heap.

11

Black Vic was breathing hard. His frustration was as intense as the midday sun beating down on him. He punched the dashboard again for the sixth or seventh time. It didn't matter how many times he had struck out at the car, it did nothing to relieve him of his anger. With as many bullets as he had fired through the house, he found it hard to believe that he didn't kill Duke. He didn't even know if he had wounded Duke.

What he was certain of was that Duke had shot back at them. The mess in the back seat of the car was proof of that. A testament to Duke's ability to aim a gun. Black Vic looked over the back seat towards the remains of Bingo. Duke had gotten a good shot, and now because of that, the insides of Bingo's head were now liberally applied across the interior of the backseat, the roof, the rear window, and both back windows. This didn't include the bit that had hit him and Echo.

The bullet had come through the back passenger window and took off the top of Bingo's head. There was not much left to identify him facially. Identification, at this point, could not even be made using dental records. There just was not enough of his head left in one piece. The only way that Bingo would be identified would be through his gang tattoos because Black Vic was going to make sure that the body had no finger prints.

If Bingo was allowed a burial, he would have needed a closed casket but Black Vic was not about to even allow that much. The many gang tattoos would not be an issue anymore either after Black Vic gave Echo his instructions. What he had planned would take care of most questions, or at least have another police department ask questions with no easy answers to them.

Black Vic looked over at Bingo and said, "Take da car down ta Savannah and ditch it. Take somma' of dat sulfuric acid 'n burn off Bingo's finger tips and tats. Burn the car after dat, wit' him in it."

"Won't da Savannah po-po find out dat car came from Atlanta?"

"No, fool. Da car was lifted in Tennessee. Take da tags off and we good. I'll send down a car ta get chu. 'Fore you leave, get a burner phone and drop you and Bingo's phone in da acid."

"So what chu gone be doin, Black Vic?"

A dark shadow passed over Black Vic's face as he thought back on his failure to kill Duke and then having to run off without having accomplished his goal. This was going to be the second time around that Duke made him look like a fool. Everyone on the street, who knew what was really going on, would know that he had hit Duke.

They would also all know that Black Vic had failed to kill him. He was at risk now, in a major way. As long as Duke was still alive, he would come looking for payback for the attempt on his life. Black Vic wanted to establish an alibi as soon as possible. Not that Duke would believe it, but if he could get rid of Duke, he would still have to deal with the police asking questions.

"I left my burner phone over at Miranda's. You know da number, right?" asked Black Vic. Echo indicated that he did know the phone number of Black Vic's burner phone.

Black Vic pulled the cell phone he had on him out of his pocket. He took the battery out of it and tossed it on the seat between him and Echo."Burn dis one in acid too."

"Cool. I got cha. What now though?" asked Echo.

"Damn, stupid. Drop me at Miranda's and bounce. Do what da fuck I said 'bout da damn car and Bingo," said Black Vic yelled as he hitched a thumb towards the backseat of the car.

Echo said nothing. He took the next turn and drove them to Miranda's apartment. Black Vic gave Echo a wad of cash before he got out of the car.

"Don't get caught," Black Vic instructed Echo before he watched the other drive off into the coming night.

BLACK Vic went upstairs to Miranda's apartment when he could no longer see the car driving off with Echo and the remains of Bingo in the back seat. The hollow sound of heavy boots echoed hollowly on the concrete slabs that served as stairs for the apartment levels. She was surprised when she answered the door and saw Black Vic standing on her doorstep. The surprise came because Black Vic would always call her before he came over. He was not the kind of person to just show up unannounced and unexpected anywhere.

She let Black Vic into the apartment and closed the door afterwards. Black Vic's entrance into Miranda's apartment cast a long shadow across the room, a contrast to the fading sunlight that seeped through the windows. Once she secured the deadbolt to home in the door frame, she turned to face Black Vic and ask him why he had decided to just show up at her place.

"What's up, Black Vic?"

"Nuthin', bae," said Black Vic. "How you doin', ma?"

Miranda shrugged and went into her kitchen.

"Look, ma, I'mma need chu to tell people I been wit chu all day."

Miranda poked her head back out of the kitchen. "Why," she asked curiously. "What did you do?"

"Nuthin', ma. I just need chu to say I was here is all."

"I can't do that, Black Vic," said Miranda as she came out of the kitchen with a cup of coffee in hand.

Black Vic was making himself comfortable on the couch and asked, "why can't chu do that?"

"Sunny was over here this morning for a while before he left to go over to Duke's house," said Miranda as she sat down beside Black Vic on the sofa. She lifted her feet up off of the floor and he let her place them on his lap

"Yo homeboy was *here*?" asked Black Vic as he pointed down towards the floor.

"Yeah."

"And he went over ta see Duke?"

"Yeah."

"Damn, dat's fucked," said Black Vic while he was shaking his head.

"What's going on, Black Vic?" asked Miranda curiously with a look of concern spreading across her face. "And what the hell is all over you?"

"Nuthin'," said Black Vic as he ducked his head to keep her from looking into his eyes and face. He had tired to clean up the bits and pieces of Bingo off of him but he guessed that he missed some blood somewhere on him. "I just hope yo homeboy wasn't there."

"Wasn't where?" asked Miranda with a hint of panic now creeping into her voice. "What did you do, Black Vic?"

"I ain't do nuthin', 'member? I been wit chu all day."

"Quit playing games, Victorious. What's so bad about Sunny being over at Duke's place," asked Miranda desperately.

The panic in her voice was an undertone for her panic by this time that emphasized her concern for Sunny. She took her feet out of Black Vic's lap and set them on the floor. She sat up straight to better see Black Vic.

"Duke's place got sprayed. Looks like some of dat cheese wit' the holes in it, you know?"

Miranda's eyes widened and she scrambled up to get her phone from the table beside the couch. She unlocked it and started scrolling through her most recent messages.

'Maybe yo homeboy wasn't dere when it went down," said Black Vic with obviously fake concern in his voice.

"How do you know that?" demanded Miranda. There was a *definite* fear in Miranda's voice now. "How do you know if he was there or not?" she threw at Black Vic.

Black Vic didn't respond. He turned and started watching the television as if he hadn't said anything at all.

Miranda stood up and started pacing the floor as she called Sunny's cell phone. She tapped her foot on the floor impatiently as the phone rang and she waited for the call to be answered. It was not too long before the call was answered.

"Hello, Sunny?" Miranda rushed to say into the phone desperately.

It was not Sunny's voice that she heard on the phone responding to her inquiry. It was another man whose voice she didn't recognize. She had never spoken to Duke before but she assumed that it was he that had answered Sunny's phone. She didn't want to take the chance of being mistaken because of an assumption, so she asked who it was that she was speaking to to make sure that she was correct with her guess.

"Who is this?"

"My name's Duke. You Sunny's friend Miranda, right?"

Miranda was tempted to ask Duke how he knew who she was but given that she knew how Sunny was, she knew he would have at least spoken of her in passing, even if he hadn't mentioned Duke to her at first. She thought that he would have done that and then she realized that it was just as likely that he had read her name when it came up on the caller identification on Sunny's phone.

"Yeah, I'm Miranda. Can I speak to Sunny? Is he there?" asked Miranda but her question was followed by silence from the other end of the line.

This silence gave Miranda pause. She became a little more anxious, believing that the silence, and the pause, could not portent anything good — as far as she was concerned.

"Um, I don't know how ta say dis...," began Duke before Miranda shouted over him.

"Where is Sunny?"

"He's in surgery," said Duke quickly. When he was sure that Miranda was not immediately going to ask him a followup question, he kept talking. Miranda listened in shocked silence. "Somebody did a drive by on my house. Sunny got hit. I got 'em to Grady emergency room and dey got 'em up in surgery right now."

"Where did he get shot?" asked Miranda slowly with a voice that sounded dead and devoid of emotion.

"He got shot at my house."

"No, you jack ass. *Where* on his *body* was Sunny shot?"

"He got shot in da chest. His right lung collapsed."

"Did they say if he was going to make it?

Duke didn't answer right off. Miranda thought that she heard Duke sniffle before he spoke again. "Yeah. He gone be a'ight. They just had to put 'em on a ventilator so dey could get his lung fixed up."

"How long has he been in surgery?"

"I don't really know. Maybe fifteen or twenty minutes. Maybe more. I'm not sure."

"Alright," said Miranda as she looked over at Black Vic before asking her next question. "Do you know who did it?"

"Yeah. A nigga named Vic."

"You mean Black Vic?" asked Miranda as she scowled at Black Vic still sitting on her couch.

"Yeah, dat's da nigga. You know dat fool?"

"I just know *of* him. Look, I'm gonna call Sunny's dad and let him know what's going on with Sunny. Keep his phone with you in case we need to get in touch with you." Miranda hung up her phone and stared Black Vic down. She threw her phone at him and hit him in the chest.

"What did you do, Black Vic? What did you do?" cried Miranda.

She had closed the distance between her and Black Vic and was beating on his chest with her small fists as she continued to scream the question at him. Black Vic grabbed Miranda's wrists to stop her from hitting him. He cast her to the side, causing her to fall onto the couch. She crumpled on the back of the couch and cried.

"Crazy bitch," yelled Black Vic. "Look what he done to my *face*."

Miranda stopped crying long enough to really get a look at Black Vic. She had noticed the black eye and the puffiness when he came in, but she thought nothing of it beyond the thought of him getting into a fight that might have gotten the better of him a little bit. She had already accepted the fact that he was a thug and in a gang so she just assumed that the look of his face had something to do with that. Sunny told her that Black Vic and Duke had fought but she had no idea that the way that Black Vic looked now had anything to do with that fight because Sunny left out the details.

"What did you do to my friend?" Miranda hissed. She refused to acknowledge the damage that she saw had been done to Black Vic's face. She was more concerned about Sunny and at the moment could give less than a damn about Black Vic. She would not have given up a bent nickel to save his ass right then. That was how little she cared.

"I shot da house up. I was hoping ta kill Duke but I didn't. He took out Bingo."

"I could give two fucks about Bingo. I wouldn't have even given a shit if he had killed your dumb ass. You hurt Sunny."

Black Vic raised his hand at Miranda. "Watch cho mouth, bitch," he threatened.

Miranda jutted out her chin and said, "or what?"

She waited. Black Vic eventually backed down and lowered his hand. The fire had gone out of him. It was due to the emotional drain from the last few hours. He was coming down off an adrenaline high.

"I thought so," said Miranda as she got up and picked up her phone.

She went back into her bedroom and came back out momentarily, wearing a pair of jeans and a t-shirt. She had answered the door earlier while wearing only a pair of panties and a cut off t-shirt. Miranda had her wallet and keys in one hand and was dialing a number on her phone with her other hand. The phone rang on the other end and was answered; Miranda began speaking.

"Yeah, dad? It's me, Miranda... Sunny's been shot... he's at Grady Hospital right now... Yeah, he's in surgery... I'll meet you there then."

Miranda hung up the phone and stared at Black Vic until he got uncomfortable and looked away from her intense and piercing stare. She made a rude noise and walked out of the front door of her apartment, leaving Black Vic behind. Alone. Right where he was, in the center of her living room.

DUKE was waiting for Miranda at the entrance of the hospital by the time she got to Grady Memorial Hospital in downtown Atlanta. Miranda found herself squinting as she walked toward Duke, the sun's brilliance momentarily blinding her and emphasizing her uncertainty about the encounter. She didn't know how she should greet him, considering that she only knew of him from his reputation and from what Sunny told her of him. She knew that Sunny was supposed to have broken up with him earlier in the day as well so that didn't make things any easier either when trying to figure out how to greet him. It was rather awkward for her so she just figured it would be easier to just think about Sunny. After all, Sunny was the reason that she was there meeting with Duke in the first place.

"Is Sunny okay?" Miranda asked.

"From what I was told after I got off the phone wit chu, he gone be outta surgery soon," Duke replied.

"That's good. I hope we'll be able to see him," said Miranda.

"I think da cops gone try and talk to 'em first. They came at me so I just told 'em someone came by shooting up my crib."

"Wow. Is that so?" Miranda asked sarcastically.

"Yeah," said Duke with attitude. "It's like dat."

Miranda put up a hand to ward off further hostilities from Duke. "It's all good. Calm down," she said.

Miranda took a seat in a nearby chair of the waiting room that they had just entered. There were a few other people that were there as well but the room was rather big and they were on the other side of the space, away from where Miranda was sitting and where Duke hovered over her.

"Duke, Sunny's dad will be here soon. I don't think you should be here when he arrives."

Duke was taken aback, but he understood where Miranda was coming from so he played it cool and didn't get upset at her suggestion that he leave. Sunny's father didn't need to know that Sunny was involved with a gangbanger and one of the biggest drug dealers in the entire city of Atlanta. Besides, he had other commitments that he could see to now that he knew that Sunny was going to make it. Now he could worry about the person who had done this. The person who had made it necessary for him to bring Sunny to the hospital in the first place. Now he could focus on Black Vic, find out where in the city he had picked to hide, and then kill him.

"You right," said Duke. "I need to go. I gotta go and find Black Vic anyway."

Miranda looked up at Duke. "Why are you going to find Black Vic?"

"Cuz I'm gonna smoke dat nigga, dat's why."

"For real?" asked Miranda in a shocked tone, full of disdain. "You're going to go look for him so that you can kill him?"

"Yeah. Dat stupid nigga got it comin'."

"Why?" Miranda asked. "Sunny got shot behind you and Black Vic. You've already killed Bingo, so what more do you want? You still want to kill Black Vic as well?"

Duke cocked his head to the side and stared at Miranda. He might be from the hood, with only a high school education that he didn't even finish, but he was by no means stupid. The way he chose to speak was just that, a choice. It made others underestimate him and he liked that advantage.

If he had been given the opportunity for an IQ test, he would have scored very high. What Miranda had just said had piqued his interest. It was obvious to Duke that Miranda had no idea of what she had just said. What she had just given away. She had no idea of the significance of the meaning of the words that she had just spoken. Duke focused on Miranda with narrowed eyes as he scrutinized her.

"I thought you said you didn't know Black Vic? What's that now? Seems like you do," Duke finally asked without resorting to speaking in broken English. It was a change that slipped right past Miranda's awareness.

"What do you mean?" Miranda asked, trying to recall what she had said that might have tipped Duke off.

"You said you didn't know Black Vic but you know Bingo got killed," said Duke, eyes narrowing conspicuously. "That just happened a couple hours ago. How do you know so quick but you don't know Black Vic?"

"I... I...," Miranda stammered. She knew that she was caught in her lie. There was nothing that she was going to be able to say that was going to help her recover from her error.

"Where is he, Miranda?" asked Duke through clenched teeth. A lust for blood and payback exuded from him.

Miranda tried to stall for time but was not certain what she was doing it for or expecting to come along that she would need to make up time for it to happen.

"I don't know what you mean," said Miranda eventually with no conviction in her voice.

Miranda avoided making any eye contact altogether with Duke, lest he look at her and learn more of the truth. Like he might be able to actually discern Black Vic's current location from the look in her eyes alone. She didn't think that it would be possible for Duke to learn that the last time that she saw Black Vic was at her apartment twenty minutes ago, just from looking into her eyes.

She was sure that it could not be done but she was not willing to take any chances on a bet like that, especially given her most recent track record. Miranda felt that it was best to avoid eye contact and, therefore, limit the chance of the disclosure of information that would very likely lead to a confrontation between Duke and Black Vic.

Unfortunately for Miranda, Duke was more determined to find out Black Vic's location than she was of keeping the information from him. There was also the fact that he was more than willing to use force in order to get the information that he wanted. There was no doubting in Miranda's mind about the fact that he would use force and hurt her to get the information if he needed to.

If a liberal dose of violence, with a judicious and generous application of the same, could affect the outcome that Duke desired, then that was what he was more likely to employ as a means of encouraging cooperation between others and himself. It had been working well enough for him for years. Even with mixed results, it was still an effective means to get lips moving and tongues wagging.

Even with mixed results, he would still gain satisfaction from the act alone. He was pretty certain that using a bit of that knowledge of violence in this situation would get him what it was that he wanted. He stepped up close to Miranda. He was ready to strike her if she gave him a reason to. In some ways, he was hoping that she would because he wanted to strike out at anything right then.

"Stop playing wit me, bitch," threatened Duke in a tight voice. He stopped and took a deep breath, backing away from Miranda a bit to give her breathing room and to allow her to feel less intimidated by his persence.

He thought about things for a quick second and made up his mind to try and appeal to her in another way. He was not a total monster after all. "That's yo homeboy in there gettin' fixed up. That nigga Black Vic did that to 'em and he's got what's comin' to him."

Miranda looked torn between letting Black Vic get punished for what had happened to Sunny and dealing with the knowledge that it was a very sure thing that Duke was going to kill Black Vic. She didn't know if she could live with knowing that she had been directly responsible for the death of another person; even someone as well deserving as Black Vic. As much as she wanted him to pay for his part in what had happened to Sunny, it just was not in her to do such a thing in this particular way.

She thought it would be better if she let the justice system handle this complicated issue. That was what they are there to do. They would at least make a decision supposedly based on the law and not based on emotion like Duke was going to do. Miranda looked up at Duke and she knew that she was not going to tell him where Black Vic was. She was also aware that her decision not to tell Duke where Black Vic was located was going to cost her. She was certain that it would not matter to Duke that they were in a public space, he was going to strike her.

"Bitch, if you don't tell me —," said Duke softly through his clenched teeth until he was cut off.

"Is everything alright here, Miranda?" asked a voice that Miranda instantly recognized.

Miranda looked past Duke and saw Peter, Sunny's father, approaching the area where she and Duke were.

"Mr. Bright," she called out with obvious relief sunk into the worry that masked her normal disposition. Peter picked up on that.

"Yeah, everything is fine. This is a friend of mine. He was just leaving," Miranda said while she pointedly looked at Duke and hoped that he got the hint that his presence was no longer required or wanted. That he should take the opportunity presented and leave.

Duke did just that. He got the real message. The message that he was not going to be able to force Miranda to tell him where Black Vic was. As much as he wanted that information, he was going to remain patient. He did have an idea of where he could start his search for Black Vic. He was of the opinion that Black Vic might have gone to ground at Miranda's place. It was the only place that Black Vic could pick that Duke would not have though of. If Miranda knew that Bingo was dead, the only person who could have told her the news that quickly was Black Vic himself.

All he had to do was find out where Miranda lived. He was not too worried about finding out that information. There were plenty of people who would know that and be willing to tell him with him using force. He just had to find the right person to ask. It was not going to be that difficult at all. It might take some time but he was going to get the information, one way or another. He tossed Sunny's phone to Miranda and walked off after he gave her a fear inspiring facial expression letting her know that things hadn't ended between them. They had only just begun.

Peter watched Duke as he walked off before he looked back at Miranda and said, "are you sure that he was a friend?"

Miranda's shoulders slumped as the tension drained out of her body and allowed her to unwind, at least a bit. Being at the hospital because of Sunny needing medical help kept her from being able to fully relax, but she was, at the least, thankful that she didn't have to worry about Duke threatening her anymore. She could cease worrying about Black Vic getting killed because she said something stupid about where he was located.

"He wasn't a good friend," said Miranda cryptically.

She and Sunny's dad sat in the waiting area until they were able to join Sunny in his recovery room as he convalesced. The hospital staff allowed visitation after Sunny had been observed for a set amount of time following his surgery. He was still medicated for pain but he was not as heavily sedated as he had been.

Sunny felt as if someone had taken a sledge hammer and hit him in the chest with it. He could have sworn that a car drove into his chest and decided to park on top of his rib cage. It hurt him to breath but he was grateful that he was around to feel that pain. It just served to remind him that he was still up amongst the living of this world — for at least a little more time.

Sunny was happy that two of his favorite people in the world were with him in his recovery room when he finally got to the point where he could make out what was going on in the world. Sunny was glad to get a gentle hug from his dad and from Miranda. Peter and Miranda didn't overburden Sunny with conversation that required that he speak more than absolutely necessary. With his chest being the source of his pain, he was glad of that. Even the act of breathing caused him considerable pain.

Peter and Miranda talked softly among themselves and their voices, along with a combination of the pain medication, eventually lulled Sunny off to sleep. His even breathing didn't sound as labored or difficult for him while he was asleep. Miranda decided to broach a serious topic with Peter to see if she could understand what was going on with Peter's attitude with his son.

"Dad, I gotta ask you a question. Do you mind?"

Peter regarded Miranda from the other side of the bed that Sunny occupied and said, "I don't mind. What do you want to know? I'll answer as best I can."

Miranda thought about what she wanted to ask again. She didn't want to upset Sunny's father, but there was no other way to broach the topic that she wanted to discuss with him. The only viable option was to just ask the question directly and to hope for the best. She wanted him to be open to wanting to discuss the subject so that she could come to some kind of an understanding. Based on the response that he would give. Miranda took a breath and jumped into the cold water, feet first.

"Why do you have a problem with Sunny?"

Peter's eyebrows scrunched up together. "What in the world do you mean? I don't have a problem with my son."

"Well...you seem to have a problem that he's gay."

"What gave you that idea?" asked Peter indignantly. Peter was just about to fall over the edge of being 'put off' by the direction he was thinking that their conversation was headed to.

"When I was over for breakfast and you mentioned to Sunny that the content of his act had something to do with him being gay. He also told me about this morning. There's also the fact that you don't seem comfortable around him anymore."

"Is that what you think?" asked Peter. "You think I have a problem with my son being gay, Miranda?"

"Well, yeah. Both of us have talked about it. We just thought —,"

"You thought what?" Peter demanded testily while interrupting Miranda. "I can't believe that you two actually think that of me."

"So it's not true, dad?"

"No it's not true. I'm uncomfortable around Sunny because I feel like I let him down. We didn't find his mother's cancer before it was too late to do anything about it. Now he has to live on without his mother in his life. I blame myself for that. As for his comedy routine, I don't want people to think that he's just saying he's gay to set himself apart from other comedians. I want him to be known as being funny and real and that his choice in the partner he takes is real and not a lie."

"Oh," said Miranda quickly. "Well, what about what you said to him this morning? If I remember what he told me, he said that you told him you didn't want that type of behavior in your house."

"My idiot of a son decided to have a fit before I could finish making my point. I could care less who he sleeps with. That was not what I had an issue with. I just want him to practice safe sex. With that being said, I am not running a brothel. I will not tolerate him having sex with anyone under my roof unless he's married to them. The same would apply to you as well if you lived under my roof."

"So Sunny misunderstood you all these times? I misunderstood you?"

"Pretty much, that's the case," grumbled Peter. "If my idiot son would have stopped and listened to me when I was trying to say that, then he wouldn't have had an issue with understanding what I was trying to say. He went off, half cocked, and cut me off before I could finish talking."

"I think Sunny is going to owe you an apology."

Peter smiled and then looked down at his son laying in the hospital bed. He leaned over the hospital bed and kissed Sunny's forehead.

"He doesn't owe me anything. I think that I owe him one if I made him feel that way," Peter said softly as he began to fuss over Sunny as much as he could. "I love my son, Miranda. I'm proud of the man he has become and I'm glad that he's so strong."

Peter walked around the bed until he was next to Miranda and close enough to her to plant a kiss on her forehead as well. "I love you too, Miranda. Like the daughter I never had. If you're gonna be here for a while with Sunny, I'd appreciate it. I have to go back to the house and get some things for Sunny. I will be back as soon as I can."

Miranda smiled softly and nodded. She said, "I'll be here. I'll see you when you get back."

Miranda watched as Peter walked away. "You heard that, right?" she asked Sunny over her shoulder, her focus still on the door where Peter had exited the room.

"Yeah," replied Sunny slowly. "How'd you know I was awake?"

"I've known you a long time, boo, and I paid attention to you in all that time. I could tell."

Sunny would have laughed with Miranda but his chest was hurting him too bad for him to comfortably join in. "Thank you, Miranda. I needed to hear that," said Sunny before he drifted back to sleep.

12

Peter found Bobby sitting in his truck, parked out in front of his house, when he got home. Peter was not expecting to see Bobby again so soon. He had left the house that morning, Shortly after Sunny had stormed out and well before the trouble began that put his son in the hospital with a gunshot wound and a collapsed lung.

It seemed to Peter that Bobby had been waiting patiently for quite some time for someone to finally come back to the house. Peter could just about imagine how long that time had been because Bobby was not there when Peter had left to go to the hospital. That meant that if Bobby had arrived back at the house shortly after Peter had left, then he would have been sitting there, in front of the house, for those five to six hours that he had been gone away to the hospital to be with Sunny.

It made Peter curious about why the young man would have been so diligent in waiting patiently in front of the house for someone to return. If he hadn't contacted anyone — and he hadn't as far as Peter knew— then he would have had no idea when or if anyone would come back to the house. He could have waited all night, and been disappointed, if Peter hadn't decided to come back home to get things for Sunny that he might need. As Peter reflected on the recent events, he couldn't help but think about how important it was for his son to not let his identity be solely defined by his sexuality. Sunny was more than that, and Peter hoped that Sunny would someday realize the depth of his own character. Additionally, Peter's upbringing had instilled in him a belief in the sanctity of marriage. He believed that intimacy was a sacred bond meant to be shared between two committed individuals, and he hoped that Sunny would find that kind of commitment in his life.

Peter was able to get Bobby's attention, to let him know that someone had returned to the house, easily enough. The only thing that it had required of Peter was that he pull into the driveway of his house and get out of his vehicle. Peter waited on the porch for Bobby. Bobby approached him hesitantly and greeted him cordially enough. After the conversation that Peter had had with Miranda in Sunny's hospital room, Peter assumed that Bobby approached him the way that he did because of what had happened that morning between he and Sunny. Peter determined that he was going to have to straighten out that damnable misunderstanding again, this time with the young man in front of him instead of with Miranda and his son, Sunny.

"Hi, Mr. Bright," Bobby said.

Peter nodded and finished opening the front door of his house. He stepped off to the side. "Hey. Come on in."

Bobby hesitated just for a moment and then he mustered up enough courage to proceed into the house before Peter. Peter followed him inside of the house and closed the door and locked it. He immediately went into the kitchen.

"Come on in and grab a seat," he called out to Bobby who was still in the living room, close to the door that he had just entered the house through. "Do you want coffee," asked Peter as he rummaged through the kitchen cabinets until he was able to bring out two coffee mugs.

"Yeah, I'd like a cup."

Peter used the single serve coffee machine they had to make the first cup and followed the same procedure for the second cup. He passed the first cup of coffee off to Bobby.

"What brings you back here so soon?" asked Peter.

Bobby blushed because of how embarrassed he was for the excuse that he had to give. That was mainly because of how things had been left that morning when he went from the house. "I think I left my wallet in Sunny's room. I didn't realize it until I went looking for it so I could show my identification to get on post."

Peter took a sip of his coffee and looked at Bobby past the rim of his cup while he did. "*Did* you leave it in Sunny's room?"

"Uh, yeah. I think so."

"Hmm," Peter intoned. He set his coffee mug down. "Do you know why I was upset this morning during breakfast?"

Bobby gulped and looked down bashfully at his coffee mug that was being turned round and round in between his clasping hands. "Not really sir."

"Take a guess," said Peter, not letting up on pressuring Bobby and making him uncomfortable in the process.

"Is it because we're gay?" asked Bobby quietly, his voice pressed against his lips with little force.

Peter was still able to make out what Bobby said. "Try again, son."

Bobby looked up into Peter's gaze. His hands stopped turning the cup in circles between his clasping fingers. His forehead creased as his eyebrows were drawn together tightly on his brow, showing his confusion.

"What?" Bobby asked.

"I said, 'try again, son.'"

"I'm not certain at all why you would've been upset then if it wasn't because we had sex."

"Now you're getting warmer."

"What do you mean? I said that at first, about us being gay."

"I could care less about you being gay so what does that leave us discussing?"

Bobby was really confused and doubted that he was going to be able to pick up on what was going on quickly unless he went down the rabbit hole. "It leaves us talking about sex?" he eventually stated; it was both a statement and a question.

"That's right," Peter said as he picked up his coffee mug. He left Bobby still trying to understand what he was getting at in the way of a point. He took a deep swallow of the warm drink, thinking that it tasted like sunshine.

"I don't think I understand what it is that you're getting at, sir, when you say it like that in a vague way."

Peter put the coffee cup down with a little thump. It was not a lot of force that he used to put the cup down but the noise that it had made upon contact with the table was enough to cause Bobby to jump anyway. The conversation unfolded under the soft, dappled sunlight that filtered through the curtains, painting shifting patterns on the table between them.

"I'm not trying to be vague. I want to be very clear on this point and I want to make sure that you understand perfectly the point that I'm about to make right now to you. You and Sunny *will not* be having sex under this roof again...unless you're married," Peter said. He watched Bobby for a reaction. He waited until he got a signal that what he was saying had sunk in.

"You don't have a problem with us being gay?" Bobby asked incredulously.

"No, I don't. I've never even said anything like that in the past," Peter exclaimed. "Hell, I'm pretty sure the reason that Sunny and I are having problems is because he think's I'm homophobic."

Peter prop his arms on the table and huffed. "To tell the truth, I got a problem with him just saying that he's gay."

"What?" Bobby responded in surprise. "I thought you just said...,"

Peter waived him off. "That's the problem. I don't think either of you understand what I'm saying. I said 'I got a problem with him *just* saying he's gay. You know, like he isn't anything else. Like an athlete, a comedian, my son. It's like he's making his identity just a one dimensional aspect of himself instead of just as a *part* of the *whole*. He can't understand what I mean."

Bobby hummed to himself. "I think I understand. I also think you need to sit Sunny down and tell him yourself."

Peter sat back in his chair and looked pointedly at Bobby. "I guess I'll have to do that. Now back to what I was saying. I have a problem with sex before wedlock, so if you two are serious about being in a relationship, you'll wait until you're married before you have sex again. That, or don't think you can be *here*, under this roof, and think I'll be okay with premarital sex."

"Are you saying that you're okay with my relationship with Sunny?"

"Yes, I am. You seem like a nice enough young man and I'd like to get to know you better if you and my son plan on being in a relationship together."

"I want that. I love your son."

"Don't tell me that only, tell him too," said Peter as he stood up from the table. He coaxed Bobby up from his seat at the kitchen table. He led Bobby towards the back of the house towards Sunny's bedroom so that he could find his wallet. Peter explained that Sunny was in the hospital and what had put him there. He told Bobby this while he packed a small bag of essentials and clothes that Sunny would need while he was in the hospital.

Peter alleviated Bobby's worry and concern by letting Bobby know that Sunny had already been through surgery and that currently, he was in a hospital room recovering and that there was no longer any immediate concerns about the state of his health. Peter gave the bag to Bobby and told him how to find Sunny in the hospital. Afterwards, Peter walked Bobby to the front door of the house and sent him on his way to go and see his son.

"Hurry up before visiting hours end, son."

"Thank you, sir," Bobby said before he hopped into his truck and left to go to the hospital.

SUNNY was awake and holding a quiet conversation with Miranda when Bobby showed up at the door, holding a bouquet of flowers. Miranda saw him first and she said something in greeting to him.

"Oh my!" she exclaimed when she saw Bobby standing there with the flowers. "I think you've got a handsome visitor waiting to see you."

Sunny turned his head to look at the door and see who had come to visit him. There were only three people that he knew of that were even aware that he was in the hospital. One of those people were in the room with him, beside his bed. That was Miranda. The other one was supposed to be on his way back after picking up stuff from his home, and specifically his room. That was his dad, Peter. He had no idea where the other person was or what they were doing. The last thing that he remembered about seeing Duke had him thinking that he had said something stupid to him before everything went dark.

Bobby was the last person in the world that Sunny was thinking would be waiting outside of the door of his hospital room; waiting for permission to enter the space. Sunny was extremely pleased to see Bobby harken the portal to his room. He would have immediately jumped up out of the bed and raced over to embrace Bobby in his arms. That was not possible though, so Sunny called Bobby into the room and waited for him to cross the space and give him a hug in his big and powerful arms.

"Your dad told me that you were here. He sent me to come and see you and be with you," Bobby said as he leaned over Sunny for a kiss.

Sunny cried openly. Not because he was sad but because he was emotionally choked up from seeing the man that he was falling in love with standing in his room, ready to lend his strength and support. His love and courage. All of him. Freely. No strings attached.

Sunny wanted to get up out of that bed but that was not going to happen. It was not meant for him to great Bobby the way that his heart told him that he should have been able to greet him. The tears flowed. Sunny's tears sparkled like droplets of sunlight, reflecting the emotions that filled the room and Bobby took care of those. He kissed and then wiped away the waters coming from Sunny's heart until the waters eventually stopped flowing all together. For Sunny, it was enough. It was enough that he was to be allowed to have this wonderful man next to him right then. Other than a speedy, full recovery, there was nothing more that Sunny wanted at that moment.

Bobby sat down beside the bed and reached out to take Sunny's hand into his own. The warmth of their palms pressed firmly together reflected the warmth of their shared love.

"So my dad sent you to be with me," Sunny finally asked Bobby.

"Yeah. It was a surprise considering how things went between you two this morning. He explained to me that we had to be married in order to have sex under his roof."

Sunny smiled, and blushed, as Bobby laughed softly.

"Yeah. I know," Sunny began. "I understand a lot of things now, that I took for granted as being the truth. I wish I would have sat still long enough and listened a lot sooner. I guess it took me being shot to allow me to slow down long enough to hear what was being said to me."

"That seems to be the truth of things," said Bobby as he looked Sunny over. "I still wish it wasn't so. There had to have been a better way to slow you down. You know... put on the brakes."

"Nothing as effective as this though," said Sunny as he pointed towards his chest where he had been shot. He grimaced. Even that movement had caused his bruised chest to throb and let him know that it was not happy with the current state of affairs. The fact that Sunny had tried to play catch with a bullet.

Movement on Sunny's other side caught his eye and drew his attention towards Miranda. She had stood up. To Sunny's point of view, it appeared that she was getting ready to leave. Paying attention to Miranda reminded him that his best friend and his new lover hadn't yet been formally introduced. While Miranda had been present the first time that Sunny saw Bobby. He didn't think that the two of them had yet had the opportunity to speak to one another. He decided to remedy that oversight right then and there.

"Bobby, this is Miranda. She's my best friend and little sister all rolled up into one small package," said Sunny.

Sunny reached out his free hand and took one of Miranda's smaller hands. He gently put her hand in Bobby's hand. "Miranda, this is Bobby."

Miranda offered a quick greeting to Bobby and begged off from any further conversation, claiming that she had her own affairs that she needed to leave and attend to before she went home.

"I guess three's a crowd right now. It's nice to meet you Bobby. You take care of our guy, I've done all that I can and I've got to go and feed myself and get changed so that I can come back later."

It was only then that Sunny realized that Miranda was wearing what looked to be clothes that had quickly been thrown on. It looked like a combination from the pajamas that she had been wearing that morning when he had stopped by at her house to see her and something from her dirty clothes hamper. She was normally much more put together than she currently appeared.

Miranda smiled at Bobby as she walked past him. "I guess I'll leave you to it," she said and patted Bobby on the shoulder as she walked out. She closed the door to the room as she passed through it.

Bobby took Sunny's hand into with of his. "You know that there are better ways to get my attention. You could perhaps just *ask* for it instead of getting shot so that I *had* to give it to you."

"I wanted to make sure that I got your full attention and this seemed to be the most expedient method of doing so, sir," said Sunny with a smile on his face.

Bobby looked at Sunny's hand that he held in his own two hands. His fingers played with those of Sunny's. The humor drained away from his features gradually as a more serious mood filled the space.

Bobby cleared his throat and spoke softly to Sunny. "In all seriousness, I was terrified when your father told me about what happened to you. He eventually calmed me down when he let me know that you were through the thick of it and recovering. I just met you and I don't want you taken out of my life anytime soon."

Sunny slid his other hand towards the tangled mess of fingers that his and Bobby's hands had become. He stopped Bobby's fingers from worrying his own. "I know what you mean. I'd like to stick around and see where this thing might lead us as well. If you don't mind."

Bobby shook his head and smiled wanly. "I don't mind at all," he said, and he didn't.

He was ready to post a vigil right there beside Sunny's bed if he had to. Bobby half stood from his chair so that he could get closer to Sunny with his lips. "I really love you," he said before he kissed Sunny fully on his lips.

Sunny was trying to fully enjoy the intimacy of the act when he heard a voice, that he recognized, calling out and interrupting his and Bobby's moment.

"What da fuck is dis?" called out Duke.

Bobby jerked upright and turned to face the door. Sunny tried to look around Bobby but every adjustment to do so caused him to be in pain. In the end, he was able to get Bobby to move so that he could see the door by calling out Bobby's name and asking him to step to the side.

"What da fuck, brah?" asked Duke again. "Chu gone tell me what's goin' on here, cause from what I see, dis dude lookin' to get fucked up."

"Duke," said Sunny. "I wasn't playing games when I said I was moving on."

"So you do it like dat?" asked Duke.

"You don't care about me, Duke. Not who I really am. You treated me like an inconvenience when it suited your needs."

A nurse appeared at the door. Duke's raised voice had drawn her attention to what was going on in the room. "Excuse me, sir," she said softly. "You're going to have to keep your voice down or we're going to have to ask you to leave."

Duke looked over at the nurse. Bobby moved forward so that he could try and defuse the situation some. Bobby gently took hold of Duke's arm and was going to ask him to come into the room so that they could talk in private. In a quieter tone. Hopefully without disturbing other patients too unduly.

Duke snatched his arm out of Bobby's grip and looked at the nurse. "Bitch, fuck you and dat shit chu talkin'."

The nurse took a step back and then left the room.

Duke faced Bobby and said, "you need to keep yo damn hands off me, brah. Chu don't know me like dat and I don't wanna fuck you up."

Bobby backed off. Sunny got angry but could not raise his voice to over power Duke's tirade. It was not that he didn't think that his own voice, raised to that level, would not be able to out shine Duke's voice. It was not that he considered how it would have been a disturbance to the other patients on the floor. He was just physically incapable of doing so. In spite of this, the way in which he spoke to Duke was sufficient enough to get the other's attention.

"Talking to you is like talking to a wall. I told you that I wanted more from a relationship than you're willing or able to give. I am not letting you hold me down any longer. You had a chance to love me and now that chance is gone. Giving you that chance got me where I am now," said Sunny.

"I thought it was gonna be you and me," said Duke.

Sunny really wanted to laugh. He did give a chuckle and then he immediately regretted it. "What kind of future can I have with *you,*

Duke? Should I pick out my own casket *now* or let someone else take on that task after I'm dead?"

When Duke didn't answer, Sunny kept talking. "I can't be with you, Duke. Don't you get it?"

Duke's face was crestfallen. He began to step into the room so that he could get closer to Sunny but the nurse returned. This time, the nurse was not alone. Beside her stood two armed security guards. Duke looked first to the nurse, then to the guards that accompanied her. Finally he looked over towards Sunny. Hoping for some kind of sign or signal that Sunny was still open to discussion about their relationship. Sunny slowly turned away from him and faced the wall that was opposite of the door where Duke stood waiting for recognition. Acceptance. Duke finally got the message with no difficulties. He made a rude noise through his teeth with a 'tsk' sound.

"Fuck you and yo bitch," said Duke as he turned to leave.

The guards followed Duke out and the nurse looked in on Sunny. Sunny let her know that he didn't need her so she left and returned to her station. Duke looked at his phone as he walked to the elevator and smiled. The text message that he had received from one of his subordinates gave him some information that he wanted.

He was upset about how he was going to leave things with Sunny, but there was nothing that he was going to be able to do about that right at that moment. There was something that he was going to be able to do with the information that he had just received. He was about to give back what someone had tried to give him but where they ended up failing, Duke was not about to fail at all. He would make certain of that if it was the last thing that he did.

Bobby went to Sunny to try and comfort him. He could tell, easily, that the drama that had unfolded with him and Duke had taken it's toll, mentally, on Sunny. Bobby didn't want to see Sunny hurt in any way at all anymore, if it was within his power to actually accomplish.

He was not successful this time in that goal of his. He could not have been successful and still be there with Sunny — for Sunny.

In just the short amount of time that he had been there at the hospital and in that room with Sunny he had witnessed seeing Sunny hurt. Sunny had been injured by getting shot and now there was the mental damage and injury from what had just occurred. Bobby resolved that he would give his all to Sunny from that day forward and try to keep Sunny smiling and safe.

13

A week later, Sunny was ready to be released from the hospital. Once the doctors were certain that no infection would set in, they were more than willing to let Sunny go home to finish up his convalescence there instead of being cooped up in a hospital room. Sunny was glad to have been told that he could go home. He was getting tired of the hospital food and having to imposition Bobby with visits to a hospital room. He wanted to spend the time with Bobby in an environment that didn't have as many beeps, hisses, antiseptic smells, and friendly nurses that thought that they were such a cute couple.

Bobby kept telling Sunny that he didn't mind having to come and see him at the hospital. Sunny was not convinced of that, even though it was obvious to him because of how often Bobby was there to see him and how late he stayed with Sunny when he did come. Bobby had even spent the night a few times during the period of his hospitalization. Sunny's father kept tabs on Sunny via video calls. He claimed that there were things going on with his work as an attorney. It was eating into his time and not leaving him enough of that precious commodity to use and visit Sunny at the hospital.

Sunny was okay with that because Bobby was there. Sunny didn't think that things were unfair because of how work kept his father away from visiting him. He felt closer to his father, after his father's revelation, than he had in a very long time. What did worry Sunny the most was Miranda. She had been suspiciously out of touch since the day she left when Bobby showed up.

Sunny, at first, chalked it up to Miranda being considerate and letting Bobby occupy his time but that changed as the days progressed.

She didn't return his text messages and when he tried calling, he kept getting sent immediately to her voice mail. Sunny didn't begin to panic until the same police detectives that had questioned him on the second day that he was at the hospital showed up again and began asking after Miranda's location. They didn't answer any of Sunny's questions satisfactorily so that at the end of the week, when the doctors cleared him to go home, he was fairly biting at the bit in anticipation of getting out of there.

Sunny had spoken to his dad about Miranda's uncharacteristic behavior and the fact that the police detectives wanted to speak to her. Strangely enough, his father didn't seem to be all that concerned about what Sunny was telling him. It was like his dad didn't care and that too was odd because his dad always treated Miranda as if she were his own daughter. For him to change his feelings for her so easily was to deny that she meant anything at all to him and Sunny knew that just was not true of his father.

Waiting for Bobby to get to the hospital to take him home was not easy. This was another point of contention for Sunny. He and his father had found a way to bring the life back into their relationship but his father had insisted that Sunny let Bobby bring him home from the hospital. Sunny could not help but wonder if things with his father were as good as he thought they were or if he was deluding himself. Either way, he as going to demand a reckoning when he got home.

His father was going to have to clear somethings up before any misunderstandings derailed what they had been working to rebuild these last few days. That was not the last thing that Sunny wanted to allow to happen. He really loved his father and wanted nothing more in the entire world than to have a great relationship with him like they had in the past when his mother was still alive. Sunny could not think of any son in the world who would not want to have a relationship with his father if he could.

By the time that Bobby got to the hospital to take Sunny home, Sunny was vibrating with pent up energy and anticipation of getting away from the hospital environment and back into that personal space that he had grown up in. The space he was more comfortable being in. Sunny had to bite his tongue on the way back to his house. He was impatient and would have urged Bobby to worry about traffic laws later but decided that it would not be fair to Bobby if he urged him to do something illegal like that.

He was going to have to be patient and deal with it because there was nothing else that he was going to be able to do to make the time go any faster. He took deep breaths to steady himself. He reminded himself to temper his desire. Stress would do him no good. Stress could only serve to lengthen his already considerable recovery time

It took as long as it was supposed to take for Bobby to get Sunny to his front door. Sunny was grateful that they were able to make it to their destination safely. It had been too long in his life for safety to take a vacation, especially given the reason he had been sent to the hospital. That was likely the reason why he now was sporting a great looking bruised chest, two new holes — one from a bullet and the other from a surgery, and more pain than he wanted to deal with at the moment. He was going to have to find safety and sit it down so that they could enjoy a sincere heart to heart discussion about their continued relationship.

Sunny was met at the front door of his home by his father and he was glad of it. Peter opened the door and waited with open arms so that he could embrace his only child and bring him across the threshold. It was only after he considered what it was that he was about to do that he dropped his empty arms to his sides and settled for a greeting that was less physical. He smiled and stepped out of the way of the door so that Sunny and Bobby could enter.

He felt chagrined. It would have been a bit painful for his son to receive the hug that he wanted to give him. Peter settled for being able to give his son a kiss on the cheek instead. He saved the big hug then for Bobby, who entered the house right behind Sunny. He was carrying Sunny's bag so he was only able to receive the hug and not return it. It was definitely not because he would not have wanted to return so generous a sentiment.

Peter directed Sunny to make his way into the kitchen where they could sit around the diner table and speak while drinking coffee. Sunny took the guidance in stride and was glad to move to the kitchen in anticipation of some coffee that was not unleaded. The hospital obviously didn't believe in giving its patients coffee that contained caffeine.

Sunny rounded the corner to the kitchen with words asking if his father had heard from Miranda being barely expunged from his lips when he stopped mid sentence and mid stride in the opening of the kitchen. The subject of his worry and trepidation sat at the table that sat posted in the kitchen. She sat there with her hands wrapped loosely around the cup of coffee sitting on the table in front of her. She had a look of worry plastered about her face, topped by a weak smile that made Sunny's heart ache plaintively for her.

Sunny approached her hesitantly. Miranda looked so fragile and so vulnerable. It seemed as if she were a small, cornered animal who could scarcely decide if the one that was approaching her was either a friend or foe. Fear seemed to make it so much more difficult for her to discern the difference. The decision whether to stay or flee clung coyly about her and smothered her in hesitation like a thick wool blanket.

She eventually decided to stay still where she was and wait to see what would happen. She didn't have to wait for too long. With tears overflowing from his eyes, Sunny rushed over as quickly as his injury would allow and put one arm around her small shoulder. He could not offer a more substantial hug; it would have been too painful for him to do so.

Ten minutes later found Peter, Miranda, Bobby and Sunny seated around the table. Each one of them with a fresh cup of coffee to do with as they pleased; either drink from the bracing beverage or nurse it. There were no expectations except to be there for one another, for comfort, for companionship, and support. Sunny was so glad to see Miranda safe. It seemed as if the sun had brightened his day.

"Are you alright, Miranda?" asked Sunny eventually. "The police detectives came by and asked if I knew where you were. They wouldn't tell me why they wanted to know and I couldn't get in touch with you."

Miranda looked down at her beverage as if she could draw strength from the cup in her hands. She was a victim of her own circumstances.

"When I left the hospital, I stopped to get some food. Victorious was supposed to be waiting for me back at my place. When I got back to my apartment, I saw Duke coming down the stairs from my floor. I watched him leave. I had no idea how he found out where I lived. He asked me when we were in the hospital and I didn't tell him because Victorious was there and I didn't want any drama from that," Miranda paused.

She hadn't looked up during the entire recitation of events. She looked up now and locked her eyes onto Sunny's. "I went upstairs after I saw Duke leave. Black Vic was on the floor in my living room. He was dead. I ran. I came here to your dad and I've been here ever since." Miranda's eyes fell back to her hands. Her shoulders seemed to sag with the weight of her worries.

"When she got here, she told me what happened. I've been trying to get her to go to the police and tell them what she knows, but she's too scared to go. This Duke kid is still free in the city and there is no way to tell where he is or where he'll show up next," said Peter.

Peter reached across the table and held onto Miranda's hand to try and impart strength through the simple, gentle contact.

Sunny reached over from his seat on the opposite side of Miranda. He gave Miranda's other hand a light squeeze. Sunny's gentle squeeze on Miranda's hand felt like a sunbeam of comfort, gently dispelling her worries.

"Hey," he said, trying to get her attention. When Miranda looked at him, he felt heartsick. She appeared fragile enough that she would break from a harshly spoken word. He kept speaking.

"I think we need to talk to the police about this. I'm sure that they already have an idea of what's happened. They'll probably need for you to just provide a few details. Nothing more," Sunny finished saying softly.

"Will you be with me?" Miranda asked.

"Of course, Sweetie. I would never leave you to do something like that alone," said Sunny.

Both Peter and Bobby nodded as well. They gave Miranda their tacit assurance that they too would be there for her if she needed them.

"Alright," Miranda finally said in agreement. "We can contact them tomorrow but I won't speak to them unless I have you both there with me," said Miranda, indicating both Peter and Sunny. This pleased Sunny because he wanted Miranda to shake off the fear that was suffocating her.

They made plans to contact the detectives that had questioned Sunny in the hospital. The detectives had given him business cards with their contact information on it. He would use the information to make arrangements to meet up so that Miranda could answer any and all of their questions. Luckily for Miranda, Peter was an excellent defense attorney so she felt secure that she would be spared being implicated as a party in the sordid affair. Miranda ended up eventually feeling much better about the entire situation after she had been able to share her fears with Peter first, followed by Sunny more recently.

"I think I left my wallet out in your truck, Bobby. The business cards for the detectives were in it," Sunny mentioned to Bobby.

Bobby stood up. "Alright, I can go and get it. Let me go to the restroom first and then I'll run outside to the truck," Bobby said in response.

"I can go get it," offered Miranda.

Bobby looked at Sunny who shrugged. He looked over at Miranda. His keys were in his hand. "Are you sure? I can go when I get out and you won't have to be bothered."

Miranda stood up and stretched. She was getting her confidence back. "I can run out and be back by the time you get done in the restroom," she said as she approached Bobby and took the keys from him. "Besides, I need some air. I haven't been outside for almost a week; since I've been here having dad look after me."

Miranda smiled at Peter and gave him a wink. Bobby gave the keys over with no further argument and went to the restroom as Miranda went out to the truck to get Sunny's wallet.

Peter got up and took Sunny's coffee cup so that he could refresh it for his son. He had just placed the coffee mug in front of Sunny when Bobby came back into the kitchen. He asked Bobby if he needed a refill as well. He topped off Bobby's cup as well and all three men sat at the table and took up a conversation about Sunny's recovery schedule from that point. Sunny had a series of appointments for follow ups and check ups on the operation of his injured lung.

He also had physical therapy appointments. The doctors all expected a full recovery with no lingering effects, just a little decrease in full functionality of the affected lung. But that didn't mean that they were going to take any chances on that if they didn't have to.

They had all been talking for a good amount of time when Sunny looked around the space and then looked out beyond the kitchen into the rest of the house. He had just noticed something that made him feel a sense of unease.

DUKE reclined in his car, strategically positioned near the residence where he had discovered Sunny lived. Oddly enough, his current pursuit wasn't centered on Sunny but aimed at locating Miranda. She held the key to his predicament as a potential witness to his crime—the murder of Black Vic.

Confusion veiled Duke's understanding of Miranda's knowledge. One fact, however, remained clear: she had observed him making his exit from her apartment complex. The revelation only surfaced after word on the streets confirmed her presence during that critical moment, potentially linking him to the crime in the eyes of the authorities.

Duke's primary objective was twofold: decipher the extent of Miranda's knowledge and discern the details she had disclosed to law enforcement. Uncertainty hung in the air; if Miranda chose deception, Duke grappled with the unknown consequences. The prospect of incarceration held no terror for him; he possessed ample legitimate resources to mount a good legal defense. What haunted him was the ambiguity surrounding the charges he might face.

Complicating matters further was Duke's bubbling anger towards Sunny and his newfound love interest. However, these emotions played second fiddle to his primary concern: locating Miranda, who had mysteriously vanished from the scene. The very same grapevine that informed Duke of Miranda's witness account now guided him to her current hiding place.

The situation presented a choice: silence Miranda or coerce her into withholding information. Duke harbored a preference for the latter, a desire to avoid drastic measures if possible. Yet, the shadow of resorting to extreme actions lingered, a possible course of action he wasn't afraid to take.

After hours of patiently observing the house, Duke's vigilance bore fruit. Miranda emerged, appearing fatigued, adorned in a loose-fitting sweater and tights. She seemed oblivious to her surroundings, engrossed in the task at hand.

Seizing the opportune moment before Miranda could complete her errand and retreat into the house, Duke sprang into action. Quietly slipping out of his car, he approached Miranda from an angle that kept him concealed from her view. The cold steel of his gun pressed against the nape of her neck as he observed her freeze in apprehensive awareness. With a deft movement, Duke wrapped his hand around her waist to keep her from collapsing on the ground. Her fear had overcome her, causing her knees to buckle under the weight of fear and shock. In a matter of moments, Duke spirited Miranda away, depositing her in the front seat of his car.

"What's up, Miranda?" Duke inquired, deviating from the customary streetwise vernacular he often employed, shedding the façade of an uneducated thug. "You're a tough one to track down."

Shifting the car from its parked position, Duke guided the vehicle with one hand while keeping the gun firmly gripped in the other, its ominous presence focused on Miranda. A quick glance confirmed her unsettled expression, ensuring she remained acutely aware of the threat he posed.

Miranda, rendered speechless, felt the weight of the man beside her and the unrelenting gaze fixed on the gun he lazily cradled in his left hand.

"I asked you a question," Duke prodded.

Reluctantly tearing her eyes from the gun, Miranda locked eyes with Duke, who exuded a chilling emptiness. His gaze betrayed a lack of emotion.

"Nothing... nothing's up," Miranda stammered.

A slow smile unfurled on Duke's face. "That ain't the way I'm hearing it. Word is, you've been spreading tales, talking about seeing someone, somewhere," Duke insinuated. His words danced around his own presence, referring to the moment Miranda had spotted him at her apartment complex before Black Vic's murder. Moreover, he hinted at her potential conversations with the authorities about that crucial detail.

"I haven't told anyone anything. If I talked to the cops I would have just told them I saw you there at the complex, nothing more," Miranda murmured, her voice softening. Tears welled in the corners of her eyes, and her uneven breaths caused her chest to rise and fall rapidly.

"Stop. Just stop," Duke said gently. "You know this didn't have to unfold like this. All I wanted was to secure my bread and steer clear of trouble, but Vic just had to stir things up. To make matters worse, he drove Sunny to leave me."

Miranda held a keen awareness of the tumultuous dynamics between Sunny and Duke. She understood that Duke's actions had driven Sunny away, an insight she guarded against voicing, wary of invoking his wrath. Amidst the prevailing confusion and terror, Miranda found herself lucid enough to wonder why Duke's discourse shifted erratically from one topic to another.

Something about Duke's demeanor raised alarms. He was unusually subdued, his voice too soft, and his speech pattern surprisingly coherent—deviating from the usual streetwise cadence he adopted to blend in. While Duke's gaze had momentarily fixated on the road during their conversation, when he turned his eyes back to her, Miranda discerned an unsettling emptiness within them. 'He's not in his right mind now,' she thought apprehensively.

"Where are we going, Duke?" Miranda inquired cautiously.

Duke appeared to ponder the question before finally responding, "I don't know. I don't know what to do now."

"Um, you can let me go... you know, just drop me off here. Why don't you do that?" Miranda whispered, desperately trying to keep her voice from revealing any trace that might trigger the violence coiled within Duke.

"That ain't happening," Duke declared with a frown. Moments elapsed in silence before he spoke again. The only sounds permeating the air were the resonating echoes of rubber tires rotating on the asphalt and Miranda's deliberate, deep breaths, her attempt to stave off the impending breakdown.

"He was mine, you know. Now I gotta fend off that Hispanic dude to reclaim what's rightfully mine," Duke seemed to murmur, addressing no one in particular. His gaze remained fixed on the road ahead.

Miranda shifted her attention to the window of the car, realizing they were approaching the basketball courts. Duke eventually navigated into the parking lot and skillfully parked the vehicle. The park was sparsely populated, a far cry from its usual hustle and bustle.

"This is where we first met, you know. Me and Sunny," Duke mentioned, turning slowly to face Miranda.

Shifting in his seat, Duke turned his upper body to face Miranda. "I don't know why you went and said anything. You should have known better than to talk to the cops. Why'd you do that?"

"I didn't talk to the cops. I'm sorry, Duke. I'm scared. I won't say anything. I'll tell them I didn't see anything," Miranda pleaded, tears streaming down her cheeks.

Duke's smile unfolded slowly, devoid of any joy. Exiting the car, he left Miranda too paralyzed by fear to make a move. Circling the vehicle, he positioned himself at the passenger door, opened it, and aimed the gun at Miranda's forehead.

"Get out. I think we done talking," Duke whispered, the softness of his words sending a chill down Miranda's spine.

With hesitant compliance, Miranda adhered to Duke's instructions, reluctantly stepping out of the car, a shiver coursing through her entire frame. Her knees quivered uncontrollably, reaching a point where standing felt uncertain. Beads of sweat traced a path down her cheek as she positioned herself facing Duke, her form leaning against the open car door.

Duke's grip on reality seemed to waver as he faced Miranda, his words a chaotic dance of disjointed phrases. "Lost in this mess, can't breathe... thought I had it figured out, but now it's all slipping away.

Vic, Sunny, everything crashing in... everything slipping away. Can't let 'em take it, gotta hold on tight."

His eyes, once cold and vacant, now flickered with an unsettling mixture of desperation and paranoia. "You see, Miranda? The walls closing in and I've lost everything I wanted."

Duke's gaze dropped to his shoes, his hands cradling the sides of his head. The gun appeared incongruous as it pressed against his cheek. "Still got them fresh sneakers though," he remarked with a grim laugh.

Bending down even further, Duke squatted, intensifying his scrutiny of his shoes. Miranda, puzzled, stared blankly as he continued his meticulous examination. "Damn," Duke began, his words unfolding slowly. "I got dirt on my shoe," he muttered, his frustration evident as he wiped away the perceived blemish. Before straightening up, he tilted his head to the side, fixing an eerie gaze upon Miranda. Her confusion deepened into sobs.

"Stop it. I hate seeing bitches cry," Duke murmured, his voice lowered, resuming his upright stance. Miranda, in desperation, scanned her surroundings, seeking aid from any conceivable source, fervently hoping that someone would catch sight of the unfolding situation and intervene. Duke tenderly cupped her chin, redirecting her gaze back to his.

Raising his eyes to meet Miranda's, Duke resumed speaking, "Gotta find my way out, but chu ain't makin' dat easy. Chu da knot, da piece I gotta untangle." The disconcerting mixture of humor and desperation in his tone revealed the intricate turmoil within Duke's mind.

His speech, once calculated and measured, now spiraled into a frenzied blur. A fleeting uncertainty crossed Duke's face as he glanced around, as if searching for someone specific. "I'm in da dark. Dem shadows be closin' in. Can't let 'em see da cracks. I ain't gay," Duke spouted, his head shifting from side to side. "Still, though... I love

Sunny," he finally whispered. Miranda discerned the regression of Duke's words, reverting to the slang typical of the city streets.

Duke's gaze shifted deliberately and disconcertingly to Miranda's eyes, causing her to shiver uncontrollably, fear gnawing at her due to the uncertainty of her situation. "I gots ta keep moving. Can't let it stop. Can't ever let it stop." The disjointed phrases hung in the air, revealing Duke's unraveling psyche, a storm of irrational fears and thoughts cascading around him.

Miranda's breath caught in her throat as Duke slid the slide back on the automatic pistol, chambering a round. He pulled the hammer back and paused, aiming the gun at Miranda's head. In a swift motion, Duke's hand flew back, and the pistol came across Miranda's face. The abrupt violence shattered the tension, leaving Miranda stunned as she crumpled to her knees.

"Did either of you hear Miranda come back into the house yet?" Sunny asked Peter and Bobby.

Both of them looked at each other and then they looked at the one who had asked the question that was causing each of them alarm at that moment.

"How long has it been," asked Peter as he stood up and began moving out of the kitchen.

He was clearly heading towards the front of the house where he would then proceed outside and look for Miranda.

"It's been about fifteen minutes," said Bobby as he looked at his watch. He too was up from the table and moving towards the front of the house.

"That's too long," said Sunny.

He was not about to be outdone by Bobby and his dad. He was as quick as he could be, given the current physical state that he was in. He pushed his mind past the tight muscles in his chest protesting his hurry to catch up with Bobby and his dad.

By the time Sunny got outside, he saw his father on his cell phone. He saw Bobby standing beside the open passenger door of the truck. He watched Bobby pick his keys up out of the lawn beside the truck. Peter pulled his phone from his ear and cursed.

"She's not answering her phone," Peter said to Sunny.

Bobby came back towards where the two of them were standing. "We can drive around and see if we can find out where she could have gotten off to," he offered.

Sunny turned on Bobby and snapped. "Are you kidding? We know where she's 'gotten off to'. Duke probably has her right now!"

"We don't know that yet so why do you think that?" Bobby asked.

"The streets *talk*. How do you think he got her address? Someone probably saw her at the apartment after Duke left and told him what they saw," said Sunny.

Sunny and Peter watched Bobby walk over to his truck. He reached under the front driver's seat from across the passenger side where he was leaning in the door. He came back over to Peter and Sunny. He was carrying a semi automatic pistol. He ejected and checked the magazine. He reseated it in the gun and pulled back on the slide so that he could chamber a round in the barrel. He put the gun into a holster he had put on his belt loop after moving the selector switch to safe.

"What the hell is that?" demanded Sunny.

Bobby paused a second. He pulled his wallet out and showed Sunny a badge and identification card he hadn't shown Sunny before.

"Who the hell are you?" asked Sunny.

"I work for the Criminal Investigation Command for the Airforce. I was on an assignment investigating drugs and a dead Airman. Duke was a suspect in that death," said Bobby.

"So you've been lying to me this whole time?" asked Sunny.

"No, not really."

"What the hell is *that* supposed to mean?"

"It means that it's *complicated*," said Bobby. He raised a hand towards Sunny to forestall any further questions that could serve to derail their efforts at finding Miranda. "Sunny, you and Miranda are close, right?"

"Of course."

"You share everything, right?"

"Yeah," Sunny said hesitantly. He had no idea where this line of questions was heading.

"Does she happen to share her location on her phone with you?"

Sunny's eyes widened and seemed to light up from an inner fire that was within him. "Yes, she does," cried out Sunny as he produced his own phone from his pocket.

He opened the app and hoped that Miranda still had the feature open and active on her phone. Her location popped up on the screen of his phone, overlayed by a map of the area. She was close, according to the app.

"Where is she?" Bobby asked.

"She's at the basketball court over on Lakewood Avenue. I know where it is."

"Good," said Bobby. "Mr. Bright, you stay here just in case she comes back. Call the police and let them know what we think is going on. Tell them there is a plain clothes officer on the scene and give them my description. I don't feel like being shot by any trigger happy cops."

Bobby turned towards Sunny and said, "I guess it would be too much to ask that you remain here." In response, Sunny started walking towards the truck.

"I thought so," Bobby said as he walked around the truck and got into the driver's seat.

It didn't take them long to get to the park. They easily identified Duke's conspicuous car. It stood out because of the tint and the rims that were on it. It was not long before they were able to figure out where Duke was. They saw him sitting on a table under one of the pavilions that were next to the court. Duke saw Sunny and Bobby when they pulled into the park and came to a stop in a parking spot. He watched them walking up to him. Miranda was sitting on the bench while Duke sat on the table. From what Sunny could see, Miranda was now sporting a swollen eye and a split lip. Sunny assumed that Duke had hit her and that only served to anger Sunny immensely.

Duke pulled out the large revolver that Sunny remembered that he had. He pointed the gun at Miranda's head and pushed the barrel up against it. "That's close enough."

Bobby drew his gun and pointed it at Duke. Sunny's hands came up so that he was showing his palms towards both of them.

"Let's calm this down and talk this out," said Sunny.

"You need to let her go and put the weapon down," said Bobby at the same time that Sunny had spoken.

Duke had stood up from the table and drew Miranda up from the bench so that she was standing directly before him. He kept behind her so that he could deny giving Bobby a clear shot at him.

"Who the fuck is *you*?" Duke asked Bobby bluntly. "Why should I listen to anythang you gotta say?"

Duke backed off a few more paces and stopped. He turned to address Sunny. "Dis yo fault anyway."

"How is *that*. How the hell is this *my* fault?" Sunny demanded angrily.

"If I hadn't met chu...," began Duke before he trailed off.

Duke spoke with more confidence when he started speaking again.

"If I hadn't fell in love wit' chu dis shit wouldn't be happenin'. Dat's why I'm sayin' all dis yo fault."

"I don't see how that's my fault. You do all of these things on your own, Duke. You murdering Victorious was all on *you*."

"Naw, brah. Chu had my head all messed up," said Duke.

He pointed the gun away for a moment. Miranda saw a chance to try and get away from Duke and so she bolted. Duke turned towards Miranda and pulled his gun up. Bobby pulled the trigger on his firearm and shot Duke dead center in the chest. Duke hit the ground and the gun fell away from him. Sunny closed the distance that was between him and Duke as quickly as he could. He dropped down on the ground beside a prone Duke. Blood covered Duke's chest and he reached out to Sunny.

"I guess I found a way outta da game. I'm sorry, brah. I ain't know how ta love you," said Duke softly.

Duke coughed once and blood came up in the spittle from his mouth. He closed his eyes and let out a heavy sigh and that was the end of it for him. As the tense exchange neared its end, the sun began its descent, casting a warm, golden glow on the scene. It was as if nature itself was signaling the close of this intense chapter.

14

The Atlanta police earned a commendation for their swift response to the scene. Renowned for their promptness, they maintained constant patrols throughout the city, not particularly due to a high crime rate but as a reassuring measure for the community, ensuring assistance would be readily available.

The initial responders effectively subdued the chaos resulting from the gunfire and ensuing tragedy. In the following weeks, Miranda underwent hospitalization for her injuries, eventually receiving the green light for release. Bobby's actions were deemed fitting for the circumstances, a judgment facilitated by Peter's affiliation with the DA's office and Bobby's role in law enforcement.

Sunny harbored concerns for Miranda's recovery from the traumatic ordeal. Over the week of her hospitalization, he made frequent visits to check on her. Interestingly, her stay in the hospital wasn't solely attributed to physical injuries, as outpatient treatment could have sufficed. Healthcare providers, however, held a heightened concern for her mental well-being, apprehensive about the potential onset of PTSD due to the harrowing incident.

The sterile hospital room, bathed in the clinical glow of fluorescent lights, felt oddly suffocating as Sunny walked in, the subtle hum of medical equipment punctuating the air. Miranda, propped up by pillows, turned her tear-stained face toward the door as Sunny entered, a mixture of relief and sorrow etched in his features.

"Hey," Sunny's voice was gentle, attempting to convey both sympathy and reassurance. He pulled a chair closer to Miranda's bedside, his eyes filled with genuine concern.

The bruise on Miranda's cheek stubbornly defied the natural shade of her skin, its presence unmistakable. The darkened hue revealed a purplish tint, a vivid testament to the force that had struck her. Accompanying the discoloration, swelling had taken hold, marking the aftermath of the impact. Though the swelling around her eye had subsided, an unnatural coloring lingered, casting a shadow on the once-unblemished canvas of her features.

Sunny winced involuntarily at the sight of the inflicted damage on Miranda. A tightening sensation gripped his chest as he contemplated his own sense of powerlessness in the face of the recent violence. The memory of the threat weighed heavily on him, and a fervent wish surged within him for greater capability to shield Miranda when she needed it most. Coming to the realization that he couldn't alter the past, he settled in beside her.

Miranda offered a weak smile, her eyes still betraying the lingering fear from the recent trauma. "Sunny, I didn't expect to see you. I look a mess," she admitted, her voice wavering. Her hand, acting on its own accord, rose toward her cheek—an instinctive but feeble attempt to shield Sunny's sight of the aftermath of her violent encounter with Duke's anger.

Sunny took her hand in his, offering a silent reassurance before speaking. "Miranda, I'm sorry I wasn't there for you."

Miranda's smile dimmed momentarily as she turned away briefly. When she faced Sunny again, she spoke, "There was nothing you could do about it. I'm just glad you were there at the end when I needed you the most."

"I couldn't stay away," Sunny confessed, signifying not only his presence during the incident but also his immediate appearance by her bedside. "I needed to make sure you're okay. And I've been worried sick about you."

A pregnant silence hung in the air. Moments later, a tremor reverberated through Miranda's voice as she started recounting the harrowing experience. "Sunny, it was terrifying. Duke... he was completely unhinged. I've never seen someone like that before. He seemed like a different person." Tears streamed down her cheeks, and Sunny gently wiped them away.

Sunny's brow furrowed in concern. "What happened, Miranda, it will never happen again. You don't have to go through this alone," Sunny assured, his words encompassing not just the past incident but also her ongoing rehabilitation and recovery. "I'm here for you."

Miranda nodded, her eyes glistening with tears. "When the gunshot rang out, everything became a blur. I hid. And then you found me. I thought I was going to die, Sunny. I was so scared."

Sunny squeezed her hand tighter, his empathy evident. "I can't even imagine what you went through. But you're safe now. That's all that matters."

Miranda wiped away a tear, composing herself. "He kept talking about losing everything, shadows closing in. It was like he wasn't even there, like he'd lost himself. And then he mentioned something about reclaiming what's rightfully his."

Sunny's expression darkened at the mention of Duke's erratic behavior. "Miranda, you did the right thing by saying something about that situation; seeing him leaving where Victorious had been killed. I'm just glad you're alright."

She nodded, a shudder running through her. "Thank you for being here, Sunny. I don't know what I would've done without you."

Sunny leaned in, placing a comforting hand on her shoulder. "You don't have to thank me. I care about you, Miranda. We'll get through this together. And don't forget, you're my little sister."

Their eyes met, and in that moment, amidst the hospital room's antiseptic ambiance, a silent understanding passed between them. Sunny was a pillar of support, and Miranda, despite the trauma, found solace in his presence.

"So, Duke's dead, huh?" Miranda asked.

Sunny cast a brief glance downward at their intertwined fingers, avoiding the troubled gaze in her eyes. "Yeah. He's gone, finally. I guess that was probably the way his life was meant to end after all. Seems like a meaningless existence at this point."

"And what about you and Bobby?" Miranda asked cautiously. She had gathered enough information about the incident and those involved to discover that Bobby wasn't who either she or Sunny thought he was. He had been keeping his law enforcement role a secret.

"I don't know," Sunny admitted after a brief pause. "I haven't heard from him in these last two days. He hasn't returned my calls or texts, and honestly..." Sunny trailed off. He wasn't sure what he wanted from Bobby at this point. Confusion clouded his thoughts about whether he should be angry at Bobby for not revealing the truth and keeping things hidden.

It didn't feel right for Sunny to be completely angry at Bobby, considering their relationship had only recently started to develop. They weren't in an official relationship, so Sunny was well aware of the incongruity of getting upset about something he didn't know about Bobby.

Sunny resumed speaking, "I have to think about things. I don't know who he is, and since he isn't answering me back..." Sunny trailed off again.

Miranda drew Sunny close, enveloping him in a comforting hug. "I guess we both need comfort. We've got each other for now," Miranda said softly. "And as soon as I get out of here, we'll need to get some vanilla ice cream."

Sunny tightened his embrace, being mindful not to aggravate her injuries. They both chuckled softly, finding solace in each other's arms as laughter blended with tears.

SIX months later, Sunny was walking towards the backstage area of a sound stage for a popular television late night show. He waved to the audience he was leaving as he disappeared from their view behind thick black curtains hanging from the ceiling. Miranda was waiting for him and gave him a big hug.

"They loved you, Sunny," she said.

"I loved being out there."

"You were a natural," said Miranda. She opened up a clipboard and scanned the contents of it. "We have another show to do tomorrow. It's only an interview. It's not a full performance. After that, it's three more clubs. Are you good?"

Sunny looked at his new manager and nodded vigorously. His career had taken off unexpectedly when the story broke out about Duke. Even though he was minimally involved with any of it, people began looking him up because his name was mentioned and that was the real start to his career taking off. Sunny pulled his cell phone out of his pocket and looked at it to see if he had any messages or any missed calls. There were none so he slipped the phone back into his pants pocket as the smile that was on his face slowly slid away.

"He still hasn't called or sent a text message?" Miranda asked. She knew the answer already from seeing Sunny's expression change for the worst.

"Naw, it's alright though."

Miranda knew that even though Sunny had said those words that he didn't mean them. She noted that Sunny's thoughts never strayed too far from Bobby. Bobby came clean and explained things to Sunny. At first he just wanted to meet Sunny so he could keep an eye on Duke but things changed and he fell in love. When the entire investigation was over, Bobby did switch jobs to work as a crewman on that cargo plan he showed Sunny.

A few weeks after that, Bobby was deployed on a mission and had to leave. He didn't tell Sunny when he would return and he and

Sunny had yet to reach a decision if they were going to try and make something out of the remains of the relationship or not. Sunny was hurt and felt betrayed by Bobby's deception and that was where they had left things. That was how Sunny was feeling about everything that had happened between the two of them.

Miranda watched Sunny's disposition change. She saw the cloud of dark melancholy slip onto his handsome features and she hated it. She didn't like seeing his mood shift to this brooding existence that could serve no real purpose in his life. He deserved so much more, in her opinion.

Sunny looked over at Miranda and realized that she had read his mood from his face and was privy to his thoughts. She knew him too well. He put a smile on his face and tried to chase away the blues that had afflicted him.

"You wanna go and get something to eat somewhere?" he asked Miranda.

They were in a large metropolitan city so the chances were that there was someplace that was open that they could go to get something to eat this early in the morning.

"I'm not hungry," said Miranda as she declined the offer. "I'm rather tired and we've got to get up early to get to the airport. Why don't you just order something from room service?"

Sunny agreed and they left to go to their hotel. It didn't take them long to get back. Miranda stood outside of the door to her room saying goodnight to Sunny. Sunny's room was next to hers and he returned the sentiment. He opened the door to his room and was about to step inside when he jumped back in surprise. Bobby was just inside the door to the room.

Just as the sun rises to bring in a new day, Bobby's presence at the door marked a new beginning for Sunny. The shadows of doubt and hurt seemed to fade in the growing light of their shared affection.

Bobby was down on one knee. Sunny looked over at Miranda. She was grinning from ear to ear like the cat who ate the canary.

"You knew about this," Sunny asked Miranda.

Miranda smiled and went into her room, leaving Sunny to deal with Bobby.

"How?" Sunny asked Bobby.

"We got back early and I came here. Miranda arranged it all after your dad gave me her number so I could contact her."

"Wow, so what now?"

Bobby pulled a box out of his back pocket and popped it open. "Will you marry me?" Bobby asked Sunny.

Sunny smiled. He stepped into the room and let the door close securely behind him. He wrapped his arms around Bobby and pulled him closer.

explicitus est liber

.. ⚜ ..

https://writingfortheworldpress.com

Also by J. A. Springs

Chronicles of Cosmic Realms
Shadows of the Forgotten Void

elctrcsheepdrmwrks (Electric Sheep Dreamworks)
Blurred Vision
Fractured
Zero One

Essays in Systems and Being
Essays in Systems and Being

The Absurdities Anthology
How Not to Find Your Local Weed-Man

The Gifted
The Untamed Force
Next Exit

The Shepherd Series
The Bad Shepherd
The Good Wolf

Standalone
Sundrops
Behind the Red Door
Boundless Fragments: A Collection of Novellas and Short Stories
Fragments of Forever

Watch for more at https://authorjasprings.com.

About the Author

I'm J. A. Springs.

Father of six wonderful children. I served twenty years on active duty, living around the world and experiencing things I never imagined I would. I spent time in societies and countries I once couldn't have envisioned as part of my future. I've done a lot—and still not enough.

These days, I live quietly, accompanied by my cats, music, and an interest in writing that consumes me. I've been writing seriously since 2021. I never set out to write in a particular genre—it made more sense to write around them instead. As for goals? There aren't many. Enjoy the first cup of coffee in the morning and see what the day brings.

Read more at https://authorjasprings.com.

About the Publisher

LLC. Lancaster, PA

www.writingfortheworldpress.com

Read more at https://www.writingfortheworldpress.com.